Ashanti Saga:
Change of Plans

Alice R. O'Grady

ASHANTI SAGA:
CHANGE OF PLANS

iUniverse books may be ordered through booksellers or by contacting:

iUniverse
1663 Liberty Drive
Bloomington, IN 47403
www.iuniverse.com
1-800-Authors (1-800-288-4677)

Because of the dynamic nature of the Internet, any web addresses or
links contained in this book may have changed since publication and
may no longer be valid. The views expressed in this work are solely those
of the author and do not necessarily reflect the views of the publisher,
and the publisher hereby disclaims any responsibility for them.

ISBN: 978-1-5320-0083-6 (sc)
ISBN: 978-1-5320-0082-9 (e)

Library of Congress Control Number: 2016912972

Print information available on the last page.

iUniverse rev. date: 08/15/2016

Table of Contents

Preface... vii

Acknowledgements.. ix

Introduction... xi

Examples of Twi Day Names xiii

Chapter 1   The Clinic...1

Chapter 2   Lincoln..12

Chapter 3   The Cathedral...18

Chapter 4   Farewell 22

Chapter 5   On Board...25

Chapter 6   The Voyage..29

Chapter 7   A Dip in the Sea 31

Chapter 8   Makola Market...35

Chapter 9   Trek to Kumasi...41

Chapter 10   The Fort 44

Chapter 11   In the Forest..46

Chapter 12   Scorpions Sting...49

Chapter 13   Conversations 53

Chapter 14   David is Banished 55

Chapter 15   Unexpected Escort...60

Chapter 16   Forbidden Trysts..64

Chapter 17   Comfort's News..67

Chapter 18   Change of Plans...70

Chapter 19   Outdooring 72

Chapter 20   Telling the Family 75

Chapter 21 The Reverend's Reaction 79
Chapter 22 Smallpox! 81
Chapter 23 Farewell in the Forest 83
Chapter 24 Bad News 85
Chapter 25 Akosua's Baby 88
Chapter 26 Back to the Clinic 90
Chapter 27 A New Project 92
Chapter 28 Rehearsal 96
Chapter 29 A Thorn in the Campaign 99
Chapter 30 The Vaccination Project 101
Chapter 31 Celebration! 104

Preface

With a bow to the late geographer, Harm deBlij

If you were flying due south from England and approaching Accra International Airport, you first look down at a dry landscape and then an expanse of rich green hills. You see towns and villages dotting the forest, and roads connecting them.

You pass over a bustling interior city, with religious buildings, markets, housing, and parks. A colonial-era fort and a large mosque mark the city of Kumasi, one of Africa's most cultured, historic, exciting, and tragic places.

For a long time, Kumasi was an important center of a wide area, where important social and political processes were under way.

About 300 years ago, the Ashanti states united to resist invasion and seizure by their neighbors. This early Ashanti kingdom was based on an agreement that the *Asantehene* was king of them all.

For centuries, Ashanti prospered. Kumasi's market was said to be the largest in all of West Africa, and Ashanti arts and textiles were known far and wide, as they still are.

The Portuguese were the first Europeans to arrive on West Africa's shores, in about 1470. They called the area the Gold Coast and built forts to protect their gold trade. The Dutch drove them out, and the trade in slaves became more remunerative than the sale of gold. When the British replaced the Dutch, they controlled their trade with the help of a string of small tribes near the coastal forts. These tribes kept the British from entering the interior, so the British did not interfere as the Ashanti united and built a strong military force.

But then the Ashanti tried to control the coastal tribes. This put the Ashanti and the British in conflict, and in the first major clash, in 1824, Ashanti forces dealt the British a heavy blow and killed their Gold Coast governor.

For some time, the British apparently felt that controlling the Gold Coast was not worth the expense, and they considered leaving the Gold Coast completely. This could have happened if the Ashanti had not attacked, planning to drive the few remaining British colonizers out of the area.

London became aware of the might of the Ashanti kingdom, and British forces invaded Ashanti. They entered the capital city, and destroyed the royal palace and most of Kumasi.

The British built a large fort there to house and protect the British citizens involved in colonial management. They also arrested the *Asantehene* and his court, sending them to the Seychelle Islands, miles off the eastern coast of the African continent.

The British did not practice good leadership or management, and soon the Ashanti were organizing to confront their conquerors once again.

The story of that final uprising of 1900 is the backdrop to the first book in this series, *Ashanti Saga: The Fort*. The current novel takes place twenty-two years later, and involves descendants of some of the original characters.

With injections of British and American blood, this West African family will be followed over five generations. In 2000, the descendants of those who originally met in embattled Kumasi will meet in the shadow of the fort, affirming that they will forever honor those who set them on their multicultural journey.

Acknowledgements

During my stay in Ghana doing research for both *Ashanti Saga: The Fort* and for this novel, Nana-Kow Bondzie helped with housing and Victoria Sackey (Auntie Nana) and her family provided hospitality and companionship. The late T. Q. Armar provided transportation when needed and the artist Saka Aquaye gave me valuable comments on my writing. The staffs of the George Padmore Library and of the Ghana National Archives, both in Accra, were very helpful.

A number of my Ghanaian former students have given me useful advice, including fisheries expert Kofi Fynn-Aikins, pediatric oncologist Dr. Isaac Odame and physician and mystery writer Dr. Kwei Quartey. Many other friends have been helpful, and though unnamed, they are not unappreciated.

My greatest debt, however, is to Lawrence Stern, author of *Stage Management*. His careful reading of the text of this novel and his detailed and practical suggestions have been invaluable.

Thank you, all.

Introduction

A*shanti Saga: Change of Plans* is a historical novel. In it, the reader meets several characters who actually existed in the early twentieth century. J.B. Danquah was a Ghanaian pan-Africanist, scholar, lawyer and historian. He later opposed President Kwame Nkrumah, whom we also meet as a small boy in Accra.

The Gold Coast Aborigines Rights Protection Society Kofi Mensah supports in his efforts to give more power to Africans did exist. Formed in the 1890s by traditional African leaders and the educated Gold Coast elite to protest bills threatening land ownership, it became the main political organization leading sustained opposition against the colonial government.

Two languages are spoken by characters in this book: English and Twi (pronounced chwee), but the book is written in English. You may notice that Kofi and Comfort/Akosua sometimes appear to speak perfect English, while at other times they exhibit errors in their speech. This is because when they are speaking their own language to each other they of course speak it well, while when speaking to English-speaking people they use their second language, English, and their speech is not perfect.

A few Twi words are included in the book, and usually they are defined on the spot. However, as many readers hear words in their heads as they read, the following pronunciation and translation guide may be helpful.

Abrofo (white men): ah-BRO-fo
Akwaba (welcome): ah-KWA-buh
Bra (come): brah
Calabash: (a bowl or utensil made from the shell of a gourd)
Garden egg: (similar to an eggplant but small as an egg)
Groundnut: (peanut)
Medasi (thank you): meh-DAH-see
Medasi pi (thank you very much): meh-dah-see PEE
Mogya (flesh and blood; physical body): MO-juh
Ntoro (soul): n-TOR-oh
Obroni wawu (white man is dead, referring to second-hand clothing): oh-broh-ni WAH-woo

Two words in the Hausa language of the northern part of the country are included: kunama (scorpion) and yi maci (march!).

Examples of Twi Day names:

	Male:	Female:
Sunday:	Kwasi	Akosua
Monday:	Kodjo	Adwoa
Tuesday:	Kwabena	Abena
Wednesday:	Kwaku	Ekua
Thursday:	Yaw	Yaa
Friday:	Kofi	Afua
Saturday	Kwame	Ama

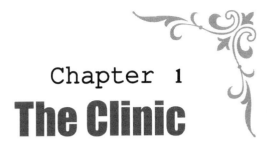

Chapter 1
The Clinic

Kofi Mensah threw open the shutters of the Kumasi Area Dispensary in Asim. The cool morning air rushed in as he removed his colorful traditional cloth and donned a white cotton coat over his khaki shorts. The whiteness of the clean coat, stiff with the cassava starch his wife made, caused his mahogany skin to look even darker. He had always been stocky, and now he had a growing paunch. Afua, his wife, said he was fat because he liked palm wine too much. But then, Kofi pointed out, she was a slim woman who never gained weight unless she was pregnant. What would she know?

Kofi inhaled the familiar smell of the lab coat, and knew his day had begun.

After putting away the clean glassware, he donned his half-glasses to check the patient log. Three patients who had arrived too late to be seen the previous afternoon were to be given priority.

When he first became a dispenser, Kofi had never turned away late-arriving patients. As a result, he often worked until dark, which consistently arrived shortly after six p.m. in a country so near to the equator. Kofi did stop work then, as there was no electricity, and he did not want to work by the poor light of kerosene lanterns.

Kofi's wife Afua was unhappy with the situation. "I never know when to expect you for your evening meal, and I worry about you walking home when snakes or other wild animals might attack you." Also, Kofi was often tired when he awoke in the mornings.

One day Afua had come home from the market with a gift for her husband. Afua explained in her native Twi language that it was to solve his problem of working late. Kofi was excited as he unwrapped the newspaper.

"What is this, my dear? A clock!"

"Yes," she said. "You simply stop taking patients when the clock shows a certain time. It won't be you denying them; it will be the timepiece."

Kofi laughed with a powerful sound that came from deep inside him. He hadn't laughed like that for a long time, and it felt good.

Ever since then, the clock had stood at the reception window, and the receptionist was instructed that when it read five p.m. she was to take the names of remaining patients and close the shutters of the window. These patients were the first to be seen the following morning,

Just before seven that morning, Kofi's saw his eldest child, Comfort, coming up the hill to the clinic, carrying a container of boiled water on her head. Comfort had been helping her mother prepare the younger children for school.

She wore her hair short, as if she were still a schoolgirl. A small dab of palm kernel grease rubbed on her hair each morning after her bath made it shiny, and picking it with a wooden comb to make it look more abundant finished the process. The comb had a carved handle; her parents had given it to her when she graduated from the Basel Mission Secondary School in Kumasi, where she had been awarded a passing-out certificate several months earlier.

As she strode up the well-worn path through the abundant wild growth, Comfort was pondering how she would accomplish her goal of compensating the Asim community for the help that many had given with her school fees. These fees were not high, but with Kofi and Afua determined that Comfort's three younger brothers also be educated, the donations were welcome. Comfort had been enrolled for twelve years, the first village child to accomplish this.

Her mother had told Kofi that she couldn't understand her daughter's ambition. "What a woman does with her life should be to marry and raise as many children as her husband can give her."

Comfort had other ideas. "Well, Mrs. Okine and Mrs. Essah at school have families, but they still teach every day." She and her mother had been washing the family laundry behind the house. Comfort threw the soapy water on the tomato plants and poured rinse water from a bucket into the pan.

Afua had never been to school. She'd learned a little English and to add and subtract in her head when she started selling in the market as a child, and felt no need for paper and pencil. Afua had declared to her husband years before that it was a mistake to educate their only daughter. "The girl will forget the traditional ways, move far away, and leave us alone in our old age," she had argued. "Educated children forget the proverb, 'If someone takes care of you until you have finished teething, you have also to take care of him after he loses his teeth.'" Afua lost the argument.

Comfort had explained to her mother, "I shall have to establish my career first, because if I were married and had children it would be difficult to get the training I need." As she rinsed each piece, her mother draped it over one of the oleander shrubs that surrounded the compound. Their neighbors laid clothing on the ground to dry, but Kofi had forbidden it because, he said, that practice led to infection by parasites.

"You know you can always leave your children with us while you go away to be trained."

"I know, but I want to raise my own children." Comfort saw the look of disappointment on her mother's face. "Forgive me, mother, but, well, I can't bear the thought of anyone, even you, rearing my children. That's something I want to do myself."

"You're reminding me of when you were just starting to talk, and we tried to feed you, or help you walk, or anything." Afua laughed. "You would push us away and say, 'Do myself.'"

To her father as they walked home from the clinic, Comfort had admitted, "I can't imagine spending my life within the confines of a family, as mother has. She has no other outlet for her energy than selling her vegetables at the Kumasi market."

"That's because her children are growing up. If she had a baby or young child to look after, that would give her life more focus," Kofi replied. "That should be the essence of a woman's life."

"Sorry, Father, but not *this* woman." Comfort felt she needed a broader horizon. "For some time I thought that teaching was the path for me, but now I've changed my mind."

Comfort and Kofi were chatting during the lunch break they took each day. Comfort had closed the reception window, and they talked as they walked down the hill toward home.

It was always a hot meal, as were all meals in the Ashanti culture, and today Afua had prepared bean stew and kenkey. The kenkey was nice and sour, the way Kofi liked it. Afua had allowed the balls of fermenting ground corn to stand for several days before steaming. The family didn't talk while they ate, but Kofi and his daughter's walks to and from the clinic afforded time for conversation.

Comfort continued their conversation as they returned to the clinic. "When the mission school closed during that terrible influenza epidemic and I helped you at the clinic, my interest in the medical profession was aroused."

"I suspected that. You know, the school in Nigeria where I qualified as a dispenser also trains nurses. I could try to get you admitted there."

"Oh, Father, I would appreciate that."

Kofi had been as good as his word, and his detailed letter to the training school along with Comfort's graduation certificate had resulted in a letter of admission for January of the following year. Comfort was overjoyed with the news. "Oh, *medasi*, thank you, Father. I want to serve our neighbors as a nurse right here in Asim. Until January, I'll stay here helping at the clinic."

In the meantime, Kofi was happy to have his daughter close to him. She was a very attractive girl, and he didn't like the idea of her working in proximity with young men. Comfort was tall for an Ashanti and had her father's dark skin. Her pretty face was distinguished by its pointed chin, and Kofi had often wondered which ancestor had given that to her. Her neck had a characteristic considered beautiful among Africans: she had neck rings.

These were what in an obese woman might be considered rolls of fat. But she was slim—not skinny like the European women in magazines—and had very pleasing curves. He knew what such a body could do to a young man, remembering how tempted he had been by that of his childhood friend, Trudi. When he looked back on his youth, he was amazed that he could have been attracted to a white girl. However, he still treasured the portrait she had painted of him.

One morning, while Comfort registered the early patients, Kofi stood on the veranda of the hilltop dispensary, a mud brick structure, whitewashed inside and out. Kofi could hear sounds of villagers cooking, eating breakfast and preparing for the day, and he pushed his glasses up on his forehead and looked over the hibiscus hedge onto Asim. He glimpsed his neighbor taking a morning shower behind his house, pouring water over his body from a calabash. Kofi looked away, knowing he had invaded his neighbor's privacy. He stroked his chin as he remembered how Asim had looked from this same hill when he came home from Kumasi after the war. He had helped rebuild the village; it was much larger now.

"Larger than what?" Comfort was standing next to him.

"I was just thinking about the way Asim has grown, my dear. I guess I spoke aloud."

"I came to tell you your first patient is waiting in your office. Here is his card." Comfort had noted the patient's name, age and complaint, as well as the date.

Taking the card, Kofi went to see his patient, who had a deep tropical ulcer on his leg. He had been cutting elephant grass with a machete on his farm, and had accidentally cut himself. Now it was an open sore to which flies were attracted as soon as the rag he wore around it was removed. It was so deep that Kofi glimpsed bone amid the festering flesh. He looked at the patient over his glasses. "Have you done anything to relieve this?"

"I took a purgative, sir, but it didn't help."

Kofi had found in many patients this uncanny faith in the influence of the bowels over the rest of the body, and lowered his head to hide a smile. "I'll give you some copper sulfate powder, which should help a bit more. Put the powder on a clean dressing, as I am doing, every morning and evening. And when you wash the bandages, boil them for fifteen minutes to kill the germs, and place them in the sun to dry. Don't lay them on the ground," Kofi quickly added as he tied the dressing in place. "If it hasn't started to improve by next market day, come back to me, you hear?"

Though tropical ulcers were fairly common, Kofi always treated them with gravity. His cousin Kwabena had developed one on his arm, and had not treated it early on, thinking it would heal by itself. He finally went to an herbalist, but by that time, blood poisoning had set in. Kwabena died soon after.

Kwabena's father would have been able to advise Kwabena, but his father was dead. Kofi had always felt guilty that he hadn't been there to help his cousin, but he had been in Nigeria on the dispenser training course.

Kofi missed his cousin. Kwabena represented the unspoiled Africans for whom Kofi had been striving all these years. It was

Kwabena's culture the *abrofo*, the white men, were trying to destroy.

"*Medasi pi.* Thank you very much." The grateful patient took the bandages and the powder Kofi had wrapped in a cone of newspaper, and slowly limped away.

It was already warm in the clinic, and Kofi wiped his round face and took a drink from a calabash of boiled water.

The next patient had a swollen leg. Kofi could see a guinea worm projecting from a hole in the old man's calf. *Dracunculiasis*, Kofi said to himself. Hardly a day goes by that I don't see it. Oh, the suffering that could be avoided by proper hygiene!

He told the patient, "As much as a year ago, you drank the egg of this worm in unclean water. Now we have to get him to come out of your leg." Kofi caught the end of the worm and attached it to a small stick, which he affixed to the leg with string. "Papa, each day you gently wind the stick a bit, to wrap the worm around it. In a month or so it will all come out. But don't pull it, as the worm will break and stay inside you. And don't immerse your leg in water that others might drink, or you could spread the disease."

All patients were asked to bring a clean glass bottle or jar for liquid medication, and the old man handed over an empty beer bottle. Kofi carefully poured a small amount of alcohol into a clean bottle, made a stopper of rolled newspaper, and gave it to the patient. "After the worm comes out, wash the wound daily with this liquid, so it doesn't become infected. And boil your water before drinking it." The man thanked Kofi and departed on the arm of his small daughter.

"Comfort! Who is next?"

"Oh, I'm sorry, Father. I didn't see that patient leave. It's a woman with a very strange-looking face. She says she has no pain, but that her face keeps getting more deformed."

"Send her in."

As soon as Kofi saw the woman, his heart sank. This was clearly a case of leprosy, previously unknown in this area. Kofi had seen it when his dispenser training class in Nigeria visited a leper colony, and the symptoms were unmistakable. There were uneven bumps where the patient's eyebrows should be, and her nose was very thick and lumpy.

"Good morning, Auntie. Tell me about this thing that is happening to you. When did it start?"

The patient recited her tale of woe in the harsh voice typical of lepers. Her voice reminded Kofi of his Uncle Mensah, whose raspy voice, it had turned out, was due to a slow-growing throat cancer that had eventually killed him.

"My eyebrows started to disappear at the end of the last rainy season. The other changes happened so slowly I almost didn't notice them. I don't have a mirror, you see." Kofi learned that she had recently arrived from the North, and was living with her sister in Kumasi.

"I'm giving you some medicine that might slow down these changes. Take one small mouthful in the morning and in the evening." He filled her bottle with chaulmoogra oil. "My dear, I would also like you to report to the Colonial Medical Officer in Kumasi, where you will be given further care." He didn't tell her that Dr. Findlay would probably have her sent to the leper colony at Ho, in British Togoland, east of the Gold Coast.

The day proceeded, with Kofi dispensing medications to some, splinting a broken arm, and referring several more patients to Dr. Findlay, the Colonial Medical Officer.

Findlay was a British doctor, and when he wasn't traveling to visit the six dispensaries in his district, he saw patients in his office in Kumasi. He had once asked if Kofi wished to be a doctor. Kofi demurred, saying, "Since I am happy with what I am doing now, why should I go away to study for six years to come back and do the same thing?"

As Kofi had related to his oldest son, Kwaku, "What I didn't mention to Dr. Findlay was that my other work, ridding the Gold Coast of the white colonialists, is too important to leave now."

Kofi was Kumasi chairman of the Gold Coast Aborigines Rights Protection Society; he conducted its meeting each Wednesday evening. This organization had been formed to oppose an attempt by the British government to take over all unoccupied land in the Gold Coast. The Society had been victorious over the British, at least on that point.

Kofi had been one of the representatives of the A.R.P.S. at the inaugural meeting of the National Congress of British West Africa in Accra two years earlier. As Kofi had explained to Afua when he returned home, "We put the British on notice that West Africans would no longer accept the colonial status quo."

An important question being discussed at A.R.P.S. meetings concerned African representation on councils and committees. Kofi reported to Afua, "Some think representation on councils and committees should be afforded to chiefs and their allies, as the British choose to do. But others argue that ordinary, non-royal Africans should represent their countrymen."

At the last meeting, Kofi had finally said, "This issue is not worth our time debating. No African should be satisfied with mere representation in the white man's groups. We should demand a complete withdrawal of the *abrofo!*"

He often wrote his opinions to The Gold Coast Nation, The Gold Coast Leader and the Twi language press, and was pleased when he saw them in print. "One outrageous matter," Kofi wrote, "is the Englishman's belief in Britain's civilizing mission. I believe that we Ashantis would be better off without the white soldiers, administrators, and traders, and I demand their ouster. Then we can go back to our own, traditional culture."

Kofi's oldest son, Kwaku, often went to the Protection Society meetings with his father. He lived in Kumasi with his wife, but he was a worry to Kofi. It seemed that Kwaku never seemed to have enough money, except to buy akpeteshie, a local gin made from by-products of sugar cane processing. Kwaku worked for a cocoa farmer, and spent much of his spare time playing in a neighborhood guitar band. They played a kind of music that Kofi liked because it sounded African, though not like any traditional Ashanti music he knew of. They called it "highlife."

Kwaku believed the white man was there to stay. "We just have to be sure he gives us fair representation on the Gold Coast Legislative Council."

On another day, Comfort brought up the subject of religion as she and Kofi walked back after lunch.

"Your rejection of Jesus weighs heavily on my heart, Father." Comfort had often spoken of this to Kofi. "But I'm pleased. . ."

"That I have only one wife," Kofi finished for her. He took off his glasses and reached below his cloth to put them in the pocket of his shorts. "I have only one wife not because the church preaches such behavior, and you know that, my dear," he retorted. "It's because I want my children to grow up knowing I am in the house."

If a man had more than one wife, he would spend time—sometimes even weeks or months—with each of them. The respective wives raised the children, some of whom seldom saw their father.

Comfort had been baptized a Christian when she was twelve. Every Sunday morning she walked the three miles to Kumasi to attend church. "Well, you know, Father, I pray daily to Jesus to save your immortal soul."

"What I know is this," her father said. "By observing our customary rites we preserve the life and fortunes of the clan." Kofi counted these off on his fingers. "Birth, naming, puberty, marriage, death, and veneration of our ancestors."

"I know, Father, but. . ."

"Honoring these properly—that is our way of life. I really don't need your prayers, thank you."

"But the Christian reverends say that we shouldn't celebrate these ceremonies in the traditional way. They say they are the work of the devil. It's so confusing! Sometimes I participate to please the family. Then I feel guilty when I go to church. As if I'm just pretending to be a Christian."

Comfort stumbled on the path, but she reached up to steady the gourd of boiled water she carried on her head, and it did not spill. "I sometimes lie awake nights, wondering if I'm to burn in hell for all my sins," she went on.

Kofi thought about this for a time. "There are things foreign priests don't know and the African priests have forgotten. Being part of community life includes family obligations."

Kofi laid his hand on his daughter's shoulder in a rare show of affection. "You are trying to live in two worlds. You participate in African society and divorce yourself from it at the same time. I don't know how to relieve the guilt you feel, but it was your choice."

"That's true, Father. Nobody forced me to become a Christian. But I didn't know it would be so difficult!"

"The ancestors and the traditional gods were good enough for Africans before the white man came. I can't help feeling that the stresses created by the presence of the *abrofo* are what make some people feel their new deity is necessary, my dear."

"Oh, Father," she laughed. "You're so old-fashioned."

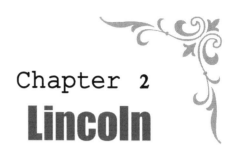

Chapter 2
Lincoln

A rare English snowstorm raged outside the windows of the Georgian house on Priorygate. The bells of Lincoln Cathedral at the top of the hill could hardly be heard through the whistling of the wind as they rang for evensong.

"Wonder if the Bentley will start. Snowdrifts'll be outrageous with this wind," Paul Hodgson said to his wife as he left her dressing room. As he glanced into a hall mirror he murmured, "Not bad for a man just three days past his forty-second birthday. No paunch, no grey hair, and I could probably still fit into the clothes I wore in Kumasi."

Paul idly kicked the swan's nest grate of the white tile fireplace in the drawing room. The soot swirled into the flames, and as Trudi entered the room, Paul told her to remind the maid to do a better job on the fireplace.

Trudi took another sip from the glass of wine she carried with her, and she responded to his last comment in her dressing room. "Nonsense, darling. With all we paid for that vehicle, it had damned well better start. I do so want to go to this dinner party. It won't hurt your reputation, either, to be seen at the finest house in Lincoln."

"Reputation, reputation. You should have thought of that when you married this poor newsman. But then, I suppose, it was more important to have an excuse not to return to the Basel Mission with your father."

"I must admit you're right, Paul. After that terrible war, I no longer trusted the Gold Coast Africans, even though I grew up with them." Trudi refilled her wine glass. At thirty-eight, her looks still turned heads. Her blonde hair was bobbed, as was the fashion, and this evening her blue eyes were set off by an evening dress decorated with bugle beads of the same shade. Only the heavy sweater she wore against the chill of the room detracted from the effect.

"May I point out that you're already unsteady on your feet? You promised not to go to social events that way."

"Oh, I'm perfectly fine." Trudi sat down heavily on a sofa. "But you had been eager enough for marriage, as I recall."

"And now, what do we have? Our marriage is just a formality, 'for the sake of the children.'" Paul shook his head, his blond hair falling over his forehead. "And you enjoy life by dallying with your portrait subjects, most recently that Liberian diplomat in Hamburg."

"That's not fair, Paul. He simply was very appreciative of my portrait."

"And you insisted the children attend boarding schools and spend school holiday time with a nanny. I hardly know them."

Earlier that evening, Trudi had knocked on the door of Paul's bedroom as he was dressing. "Come!" he cried.

"Paul, why don't we have a glass of wine with the children before leaving?"

"Hard to believe I have a son old enough to drink with." Paul smiled into the mirror as he tied his black silk bow tie. "Fatherly pride, that sort of thing."

Just that morning, Paul had been chatting with George, his assistant editor at the Lincoln Gazette. They were in Paul's office, with the door shut to keep out the bedlam of the many typewriters and telephones. George had said how proud he was of his youngest son, who had just passed his A-level exams and would soon enter university.

Paul had confessed to his assistant that he had never told anyone he was proud of either of his children. He'd considered it boasting, he said, and had shied away from it.

Looking now at his tall son David in his Sandhurst uniform as he and young Kate entered the drawing room, Paul said, "So you're soon to graduate as a second lieutenant, David. Something to be proud of."

He made a mock toast toward his son with his wine glass. Paul had told his wife several times that he preferred stout, but that was a drink of the working class, according to Trudi. So that evening, as always on such occasions, they drank wine.

David was surprised by his father's words, and smiled in appreciation.

His father glanced at the large portrait over the fireplace. It was of the two children, painted by Trudi eight years earlier. It showed David, already tall for his age, dreaming of far places and romantic scenarios, and Kate, chubby and angelic, looking with curiosity at the world.

Kate was staring into the new convex mirror between the windows. "It's like the fun mirrors at the Pier in Brighton!" she said.

"Come sit here by me, Kate." Trudi patted the seat next to her on the sofa, but Kate continued looking into the mirror.

Kate was home this weekend from her boarding school, though she would have preferred to stay there and work on her art projects. For an eleven-year-old, Kate showed impressive artistic talent, and was taking private art lessons. She had only made arrangements to come home when she learned that her brother would be there.

David stood in front of the heavy velvet window drapes, closed against the weather. His arm rested on the back of a Chippendale chair as he looked around the room at his family, impressing their images on his mind. Such a cozy scene, David thought—one would say from looking at them that they were a happy family.

He struggled to make an announcement. "Mother, Father…" He took a deep breath before going on. God, this is difficult, he thought.

For courage, and to give himself time, he took a sip of the Riesling his mother had brought back from her recent visit to Germany. David's long fingers gripped the delicate wine glass, and, fearing he might break it, he set it on the polished satinwood surface of a table next to a miniature landscape his mother had painted. Better get it over with.

David pushed back the hair that fell over his forehead. "After considering several options, I've requested assignment with the Gold Coast Regiment of the British West African Frontier Force," he blurted out. "I'll have my second lieutenant's commission, and leave on the twenty-first of June for Accra."

The only sound was the howling of the winter wind.

Trudi's mouth set in a hard line, while Paul's lips formed an inadvertent "Oh." Kate's blue eyes sparkled at her brother's announcement.

David expected a tirade from his mother, but it was Kate who responded first. "Africa! Oh, David—how exciting!" Setting her glass of orange squash on the pier table below the mirror, she ran to her brother and threw her pudgy arms around his chest, that being the highest she could reach. Her blonde curls tumbled back as she lifted her head.

"Where mother and father met—it's so romantic!" Until Kate made her enthusiastic declaration, David hadn't considered the romance of it, but he knew at once that Kate was right. There must have been romance at one time between his parents. Perhaps he was seeking romance—the romance his mother and father had found in Africa.

Trudi refilled her wine glass from her prized claret jug, another souvenir from Germany, spilling the wine as she did so. "Nonsense, Kate. It wasn't romantic at all, but a horrid experience I've tried to forget." She brushed the wine from the upholstery onto the parquet floor. "I wish we had never told you two about it—perhaps then your brother wouldn't have such foolish notions." Her voice was harsh, as was the expression on her face.

David was offended by the way his mother dismissed his plans. "It's not a foolish notion, Mother. They're looking for officers to serve in the Gold Coast, you know, especially since the yellow fever epidemic sent so many home."

His father leaned on the mantel. He pushed his thinning hair back, but it still tumbled onto his forehead. "David, there are many good reasons not to go to the Gold Coast. The Africans there are agitating against colonial power—you know what happened to us in 1900—and communications are little better now than they were then. And I don't like the idea of your rushing headlong into a yellow fever epidemic. West Africa is aptly named 'the white man's graveyard,' don't you think?"

"Oh, no, Father. I'm told there have been no new fever cases in months. It's now considered safe, and. . ."

His mother interrupted him. "That may be so, but there's still malaria and snakes and—ach!—all kinds of biting insects." Trudi shuddered at the memory.

"That's true, Mother. I'll just have to be careful."

David wished his parents would leave for their dinner party, so he didn't have to watch his mother pour yet another glass of wine. At the same time, he resented the fact that they went out so often when he and Kate were home. He suspected his mother was avoiding family gatherings.

Trudi's fingers picked at her beaded bag. She burst out, "But you can't go overseas without our permission, and we won't give it!"

David took a deep breath. "Mother," he soothed, "I don't need your permission, you know. I'm a soldier now. But I would like to have your blessing."

"Let's accept the inevitable," Paul told his wife. "David has decided that he wants to serve in the Gold Coast after he passes out of Sandhurst. Can't stop him. So let's congratulate him on the assignment and wish him well."

Trudi scoffed, "Ridiculous. I won't accept it."

Paul sighed, "Certainly wish I'd traveled more. Since Kumasi, I haven't been anywhere."

"Paris in 1916," Trudi corrected him.

"One trip in twenty-two years? Trudi, let's allow the boy to see a little of the world!"

"I'm going to miss having a big brother around." Kate relinquished her hold on David.

"Our travel editor could use some Africa copy," Paul said.

Based on the stories Paul had written about the Ashanti uprising and the flight from Kumasi, he had found a job as a reporter. His parents had been infuriated at his joining the working class. But at least he hadn't volunteered for the military during the war, as Trudi had conceded.

Paul was now the managing editor of the Lincoln Daily Times. It was a time when many newspapers were shutting down and resulting worker unrest. His talent for mollifying employees and keeping the peace, as he did at home with his wife, stood him in good stead. But Paul had never visited foreign countries as a journalist, as he had predicted years ago to Trudi when they were besieged in the Kumasi Fort.

"The Times has a travel editor?" David asked, turning to his father.

"My way of asking you to write home."

"Of course." David grinned at him. "I'll try to keep you posted without giving away any military secrets."

Chapter 3
The Cathedral

The next morning, Kate, in her nightdress, entered David's room. "You're not up yet!" she cried, shaking her brother.

His pale blue eyes opened and then shut again. "No, but if you'd leave, I could be! Something specific in mind?"

"If you'd just look out the window, you'd see why I want us to go outside. It's all white out there!"

"What time is it?" he asked. At that moment Great Tom began tolling the hour in the cathedral nearby.

As she had done since she was a small child, Kate counted the strokes. "One, two, three, four, five, six, seven, eight!"

"Good Lord, Katie. I'm on holiday, you know!" But David sat up in the bed.

As she left and slammed the door, Kate shouted "Challenge you to a snowball fight!"

Bundled up against the cold, they left the house and crossed Priorygate, the snow crunching under their feet. All was still and sparkling in the sun. The sky was clear, seemingly innocent of the previous night's fury.

As soon as they reached the cathedral yard, Kate threw a snowball at her brother, and the battle was on. One snowball hit Kate in the head. "Oh, Katie, I'm so sorry! Are you all right?"

David approached as he apologized. When Kate assured him that she hadn't been hurt, David rubbed her face with a handful of snow, and Kate screamed. Like Wedgewood china, David thought, looking at her vivid blue eyes through the flakes of snow on her lashes.

After that, Kate fought the battle in earnest, and landed several snowballs that felt icy on Paul's neck, despite his fur collar. He responded with a lion's growl and some accurate hits.

When their mittens were soggy and their fingers cold, they stood under the round Norman arches at the entrance to the cathedral. They had been raised as Presbyterians, like their mother, but the immensity and grandeur of this ancient structure had always drawn them. They shook off the snow and stamped their feet before entering the cathedral.

"Did you know those arches are almost a thousand years old?" Kate whispered.

"No, I didn't, actually," he lied. "Impressive."

The smell of burning candles and the silence of the large space, enhanced by the occasional echoing cough of a worshipper, struck them as they entered.

"Let's look at my window," Kate whispered.

"Kate's window" was the huge, round Bishop's Eye in the south transept of the cathedral. As Kate had pointed out years earlier, it was the only window in the church whose glass design was abstract.

As his sister gazed up at the bright glass, David saw tears wetting her cheeks. "What is it?" he asked.

"It's that you're going away, and I won't have anyone to talk to at home. Father's so busy at the paper, and mother . . ."

"Yes, I know. Mother finds more companionship in Bacchus than in us."

At this, Kate sobbed, and Paul put his arm around her shoulders.

lay O'Grady

"Shhh!" One of the scattered worshippers frowned and gestured.

Kate took her brother's hand and led him down the side aisle, their footsteps on the limestone floor echoing in the silence. When they were outside again, she asked him, "Are you too cold to sit on the porch?"

"I'll race you there." They ran around to the side of the cathedral, where the covered stone Galilee porch offered protection from the wind. David lifted his sister to a niche near the Bishop's Entrance, and he hitched himself up to sit next to her.

"Now, what is it?" he asked. This was the place where they talked about matters they could share with nobody else. He remembered Kate pouring out how it pained her to see their mother drunk. And all I could do was advise her to be kind, he recalled.

"David, do you plan to visit the fort in Kumasi where Mother and Father met?"

"I certainly do, if it's still there," he replied. "But I don't know when I'll be able to get to Kumasi, you know." David removed his hat and brushed the snow from his light blond hair, so like his father's.

"Please, please, will you write me all about it when you do?" Kate swung her legs and kicked the stone wall with the heels of her snow boots.

"Of course I will."

"Are some Africans artists?"

He was surprised by her question. "Well, they do create carvings and beautiful cloth. I don't know if these people are considered artists—maybe it's just religion, or custom."

"Would you try to find out? I want to do a paper for school, about whether other cultures have people like Mother, just creating art."

David promised to look into the matter.

Kate looked down at the stone floor. She asked shyly, "If I give you one of your portraits, will you take it along?"

"Of course I will. How about the one you painted of me in uniform when I was home last Christmas. May I have that?"

"You complained that the portrait showed you with a crooked smile—I thought you didn't like it!"

"Since then I've looked carefully and dispassionately in the mirror, and discovered that my smile is askew," David confessed. "And you were honest enough not to ignore it," he said as he pulled a curl peeking out from under her velvet hat. "So that's the one I want."

"To remind you of home as you lie in your steamy tent, fanned by a naked native girl."

"Katie!" David chided with a smile. "What would Mother say?"

"Is your bum getting cold?" Kate asked.

Actually, it was. David stood and lifted his sister off her perch. "Let's go home."

Chapter 4
Farewell

Trudi and Kate stood on the dock at Liverpool. The wind off the water tugged at their short skirts and flowered hats, bringing the smell of fish and oil, and the smoke from ships' stacks. Seagulls hung in the air, demanding a handout.

David's friend Porter had gone home after graduation to say goodbye to his family, who couldn't make the trip to Liverpool. Trudi, Paul, and Kate had given Porter effusive farewells on the dock in an attempt to make up for his family's absence.

Paul appeared almost stern as he wished his son well with a handshake. "Keep us informed as to what you are doing," he said.

Kate could only hug her brother as the tears ran down her cheeks. She managed to say, "Write me about everything!" before she began to sob.

As it was early morning, Trudi was sober. She had accepted her son's decision to go to the Gold Coast, and she kissed him fondly as he was about to board the ship. "Taking a look at another culture may help you appreciate your own," she told him. "Just don't trust any Africans," she whispered as she hugged him.

Trudi's eyes had a faraway look, and when they were alone on the dock, Kate asked, "What are you thinking about, Mother?"

"I once had an African friend, a good friend, at school in Kumasi. I thought he was the one African who would protect me if that were ever necessary." Trudi was whispering this to her daughter, as if it were a secret.

"There was a war, you remember we told you, and while your father and I were among those besieged in the fort, I looked out and saw him among the soldiers blockading us!"

"Was he your beau, mother?"

Trudi chuckled. "Of course not, dear. He was an African! But I did once paint his portrait, and painting the Liberian in Hamburg reminded me of him."

She was thoughtful for a moment, and then went on. "I clearly recall doing his portrait: the bright sun, colorful flowers and the company of a trusted friend."

"But Mother, you always said Africa was such a horrible experience!"

Trudi shook her head. "Only at the end, darling. It's like my experience in Hamburg has allowed me to remember all the good times I had in Africa."

Kate asked if the memories helped her paint the African in Hamburg, and her mother nodded.

"I think so. When the finished portrait was unveiled, the diplomat and his family insisted that it was quite perfect in every way. They said it somehow revealed an African temperament in the man, though nobody, including me, could explain exactly how I had achieved it."

Before Kate could ask any more questions, Paul returned from his tour of the ship.

"The *Akabo* looks like a good ship," he told them. "She's twenty years old, but seems quite fit. Has 450 horsepower engines, and she's all steel."

"Paul, you don't know anything about ships," Trudi scoffed.

"After the tour Captain Tyres gave me, I do now," he said. "Impressive. The boys have quite a nice cabin."

"I should hope so, in first class. Really, Paul, you and Porter's father are too generous, paying to upgrade them. I hope they appreciate it."

"They will, when they learn what the second class passengers are eating. I'll never forget my trip home from the Gold Coast. I, the young idealist, insisted on traveling second class over my parents' objections. The food was awful!"

"Oh, Father, that was twenty-two years ago!" Kate said.

Chapter 5
On Board

On board the Akabo, David tested his bed. "This is the cat's pajamas!" He rushed to the porthole. "And a window!"

"Rather! We even have our own w.c.!" Porter cried.

"Certainly is a cut above sleeping in the Lines, isn't it?"

David and Porter had been classmates at the Royal Military College, Sandhurst, and had been friends since their first day there. Most cadets were sons of military men, who looked down on those who didn't understand military terms or know how to ride a horse. Since Porter's father was a baker and David's a journalist, Porter and David formed a bond as school outcasts. After their two years there, the bond was stronger than ever.

"What's this?" Porter picked up a box of matches from the table between the two beds and squinted through his gold-rimmed glasses at the inscription. "British and African Steam Navigation Company, Limited. Aren't we posh?"

"Sorry, fellows, bad news." Four of their Sandhurst classmates in their khaki dress uniforms burst into the room. "New orders. You're being posted to British Cameroons, the armpit of Africa. Hot and humid. Bad luck, old chaps."

With a shout, Porter greeted them. "You brought champagne to see us off. Smashing! Sit, gentlemen, sit on the beds. I'll find more tumblers—we only have two. Have some chocolates. Our families have supplied us for the full two-year tour." As Porter exited the cabin, he called back, "Don't hit the champagne 'til I'm back with proper glasses."

A dark-skinned man had entered with the soldiers. He was dressed in worn European clothes, with no hat. David held out his hand. "We've not met. I'm Lieutenant David Hodgson." Whoever this man is, he isn't wealthy, thought David. But he looks pleasant enough.

"Please forgive me for barging in on you like this. My name is Danquah, Joseph B. Danquah. I am commonly called J.B." They shook hands. "I am studying law in London. I met your friends there, and they kindly told me they were planning to see you off for the Gold Coast. I felt compelled to accompany them. That is my home, you see."

The visiting soldiers had seated themselves on the two beds, and had opened a bottle of champagne. They were all drinking from the two glasses available. "Sorry, chaps," one of them called to David and Danquah, "we'll save some for you, when the tumblers arrive."

Ignoring his friends, David said, "I'm happy to meet you, Mr. Danquah." He pulled the two chairs into a corner away from the boisterous visitors. "Won't you sit down? I must admit I'm excited at making your acquaintance. You're the first Gold Coaster—Gold Coastian? —I've met, you know.

"I have been doing some reading, though. Have you ever heard of J. E. Casely Hayford? I found his *Ethiopia Unbound* extraordinary! About establishing an African university. Where the curriculum would be relevant to African needs and conditions."

Danquah's face lit up. "I do indeed know him. He is one of my country's premier scholars and activists. I was fortunate to attend the conference he convened two years ago in Accra."

David was intrigued. "What kind of conference was that, sir?"

"More than 50 delegates, our West African neighbors, were in attendance," Danquah replied. "It resulted in the formation of the National Congress of British West Africa, a very active organization. A zealous pan-Africanist, Hayford is."

David shook his head. "I'm sorry there's so little time for us to talk. There is much information about your country I'd like to know."

"Yes, indeed." Danquah hesitated a moment, then took an envelope from his pocket. "I do have a request for you, if it is not too much trouble. My brother is paramount chief of the town of Akim Abuakwa, and one of his wives is having a business in Accra. I understand that is where your ship is stopping. Could you possibly deliver this to her?"

Taking the envelope, David asked, "Is it something urgent? Forgive me, but I'm wondering why you haven't posted it."

Danquah shrugged. "I believe the colonial government has its eye on me. I have written some pieces criticizing their policies, you see, and they probably think of me as seditious. My letters do not always arrive."

David did not want to get involved with colonial politics, but he felt he couldn't refuse this direct request. "Very well. I see you've written her name, Dora Armar, and that she sells—what? Chickens and eggs?"

"Yes. She has a poultry farm outside Accra, and she sells at Makola Market."

Porter hurried into the room with a half dozen glass tumblers. "Borrowed them from our neighbors. Seems you have to request extras in advance. Where's the champagne? You couldn't wait to start tippling?"

Porter served them all, and just as they were drinking a toast to their alma mater, the Akabo's whistle blew for guests to go ashore. The classmates hurried out of the cabin, carrying their drinks. Mr. Danquah stayed behind, and David introduced him to Porter.

Danquah raised his glass. "I'd like to propose a toast, also. May you find happiness in the welcoming arms of my people."

"I'll drink to that," said Porter.

"Thank you," David said. "I'm so sorry we didn't meet earlier. Never fear—I shall make every effort to deliver your letter, you know." David slipped the envelope into a pocket of his uniform.

"We'd best go out and wave cheerio to the old folks," Porter suggested, leaving the cabin but taking his drink.

After saying goodbye to Mr. Danquah, David and Porter leaned over the rail, waving to their friends and David's family. David said, "This may be a final goodbye, you know. We might like the Gold Coast so much we'll stay forever!"

"Surrounded by ravishing African virgins, no doubt," Porter said.

As the ship moved away from the dock, Trudi said to Paul in a low voice, "I just hope David doesn't get involved with a native girl."

Chapter 6
The Voyage

During the several weeks of the voyage, David and Porter had a real holiday. For the first time in their lives, they were without parental or school supervision. They discovered several unmarried ladies on the ship with whom to play shuffleboard, enjoy evening musicales, and dance the Charleston in the ballroom. Porter devoted himself to a nurse, Miss Gabriela Denholm, with whom he spent much of his time.

While they were dressing for the captain's formal dinner, David accused Porter of being serious about Miss Denholm. Porter chuckled. "No, but she's serious about me. She said she's always loved redheads." He looked in the mirror and stroked his full moustache. "I'm sure this didn't hurt, either. You really should try growing one, old boy."

"I don't think it's the red hair or moustache at all, you know. I think she has a weakness for bespectacled pock-marked dwarfs!"

Porter laughed and threw a pillow at his friend. His facial scars and small stature did not appear to trouble him at all.

Invariably David and Porter slept late in the mornings, missing the breakfast sitting. The two men discovered, however, that if they spoke nicely to the galley staff, they could be served a specially prepared meal of eggs, kippers and toast.

When no young lady was available for company, they read or napped on deck in the sun. Seeking company, they found plenty of older men with whom to play poker. David and Porter's travel allowances just covered their losses.

The seasoned missionaries, colonial officers, and military and business passengers returning to their posts in the colonies were happy to tell the young newcomers about West Africa. One Lagos merchant, a Dutchman, said, "Life in West Africa is like heaven. Servants, balmy breezes and warm sunshine every day. You young chaps will love it."

Others described it more as a kind of hell, citing troublesome servants, mosquitoes, snakes and scorching heat.

David asked "What about malaria?"

One "old coaster" laughed and told him, "Just be sure to keep enough gin in your blood, laddie, and you'll never be troubled by malaria."

Chapter 7
A Dip in the Sea

David and Porter's arrival in Accra was an uneremonious one—
they swam ashore. The Akabo was anchored about 300 yards
from the beach. Passengers and baggage went over the side in
rope baskets, referred to as "mammy chairs," to be deposited in
the native surfboats that carried them and their loads through
the rough waves to the beach. A rotting rope broke as David
and Porter were being hoisted over the side of the ship, and they
plunged into the sea.

When they came to the surface, Porter shouted, "Swim for it?"
That suggestion was all David needed; for two weeks he had been
cooped up on the ship. Removing their shoes and tossing them
into a waiting surfboat, they struck off for the beach. The boatmen,
their dark skin sparkling in the sun, laughed and cheered them
on as they set out.

David was a good swimmer, but fighting the waves near the
shore turned out to be more than he'd bargained for. For a time, as
he felt his strength ebbing, he wondered if he could make it—and
the next thing he knew he was being dragged onto the sand by a
group of naked children who had been playing in the surf.

The first impression David had was of the light. It was much
more insistent than on the brightest summer day in England, as
if the sun were so much closer to the earth here. It penetrated

his closed eyelids, and he gasped as he opened his eyes. David had the feeling that he should be able to see things, and therefore understand them, much more clearly in such intense light.

The children had deposited him on the beach, and now they were crowding around, vying with each other for a close look at this pink-skinned stranger. Some of them touched his hair, fascinated by its light color and fine texture. "Thank you, thank you, thank you," David said as soon as he caught his breath. There were smiles and handshakes all around. He then joined Porter, also surrounded by a group of laughing children trying to communicate.

David noticed that Porter was not wearing his glasses. "Lost your specs?"

Reaching into a pocket, Porter pulled them out, and after trying to wipe off the water with the tails of his wet shirt, he put them on. "I stowed them before we got into the basket. Good job it was, too."

A short way up the beach were several narrow fishing canoes, each hewn from a huge log. Their sides were carved and painted with colorful designs and symbols, and their nets were full of shiny, gasping fish. The fishermen had taken these boats through the surf to deeper water, thrown out their round nets, and towed their catch in.

Crowds of bare-breasted women were haggling with the fishermen over the catch. The women wore colorful cotton cloths wrapped around their waists and reaching their ankles, and many had babies tied on their backs with similar cloth. These were fishmongers who would go into the town with trays of fish on their heads to sell their goods, fresh from the sea, in the streets and markets of Accra.

At first, David was shocked at the sight. "I've never seen women's breasts before, you know," he told Porter. "Except in those pictures we used to pass around when I was a teenager. These people don't seem in the least self-conscious. Remember the women in paintings and sculptures, modestly hiding their globes?"

The children, who had retrieved the soldiers' shoes from the boatmen, recognized the soldiers' uniforms, and pointed the way along the beach to the military headquarters. David could see it in the distance, the spray of the surf giving it an insubstantial appearance, like something in a dream.

David told Porter that the Swedes had built a fort on that site about 350 years earlier, during the heyday of the slave trade. Porter did not seem interested, but David went on anyway. "The French, before they were driven out by the return of the Portuguese, rebuilt it. Since then, the Swedes and then the Danes have captured it."

"So how do we have it now?" Porter asked.

"We purchased it! And it's still called Christiansborg Castle."

David knew that Porter had no room in his life for sentiment, so he didn't let on how thrilled he was by the sight of the venerable structure. Tall palm trees, agitated by a sea breeze, shaded the ramp that led to the black iron gate at the entrance, a dark contrast to the ancient red bricks of the walls. Its ramparts, surmounted by cannons, faced the town as well as the sea.

There was no clue that the murder of a Danish governor and a mutiny of Portuguese soldiers had taken place here. David knew the stronghold had once been captured and occupied by Africans and damaged by an earthquake. But the structure had been repaired and enlarged, and now housed the offices of the British governor of the Gold Coast Colony, where arriving officers reported. Standing on the hot sand with the sun burning his neck, David found the castle welcoming.

By the time they reached the castle, their uniforms had dried, and though disheveled, they decided to report anyway.

It turned out that David and Porter's orders had been sent to them in England, but had not reached them in time. When they appeared with no orders to present, the African clerk did not know what to do. He summoned a young British lieutenant who, after saluting and welcoming them to the Gold Coast, located the necessary information in a rusty metal filing cabinet. The two friends were told they had both been assigned to the Second Battalion of the Gold Coast Regiment of the Royal West African Frontier Force. Porter said to David, "Ripping, old boy! We'll be serving together! Ever a team, just as at Sandhurst!"

The first order of business was a cursory medical exam for each of them. "Going to Kumasi, are you?" the examining doctor asked. "There's no military doctor up there, but you'll probably get to know the colonial medical officer, Tim Findlay." The doctor thumped David's chest. "A fine doctor, and a good fellow."

They were scheduled to travel at noon the next day to their post in Kumasi. David was thrilled that he had been assigned there; he looked forward to finding out if the Kumasi Fort was still standing.

Chapter 8
Makola Market

The next day David and Porter arose before dawn from their cots in the military barracks near the beach.

"We have to find the market and deliver this letter for Mr. Danquah, you know," David said.

"You told him you'd 'make every effort.' You're not obliged."

"I feel like I am, damn it. But you don't have to go."

"No, we're in this together, old boy," Porter said. "It's a challenge. Onward!"

They followed the stream of Africans with loads of goods on their heads to the central market. Some of these people had walked much of the night to get to the market before dawn, in hopes of selling their goods and starting their journey home before the sun began its descent.

Already David felt like he was in the glass-house at Kew. It was partly the colors of the flowers, and the palm trees, but mostly the air, heavy with moisture. He noticed that the houses grew out of the soil; there was no grass to be seen.

As they walked the red dirt roads, Africans waved to them in welcome. Children stared at them, and people passing nearby smiled and said *akwaba*, which the soldiers later learned meant "welcome."

Several taxis stopped alongside them, and the drivers kindly insisted they should not be walking on the dusty road. Pedestrians agreed. White men, David and Porter gathered, rode in cars.

"What pleasant people," David commented. "I can't imagine them engaging in the bloody battles we studied at Sandhurst."

Porter grunted. "Don't fall in love with them yet. All it takes is one bad apple, old boy."

Makola Market surprised both of them by its size and its activity, especially at such an early hour. Thousands of people jostled each other, their bare feet kicking up red dust.

David saw mangoes, bananas, pawpaw, and some tropical fruits that he had never seen before. The neat conical stacks were even more brightly colored than the cloths worn by the Africans.

He was assured by the seller that the green oranges were ripe in spite of their color, and was given one to taste. The seller had cut off one end so they could squeeze it and drink the juice, as the Africans did. But instead, David and Porter tore off the skin and ate it in sections, attracting the attention of the Africans around them. Both men agreed that is was ripe, and delicious.

Porter bought a basket of oranges from the seller. When he briefly balanced it on his head, the market women screamed with approving laughter and clapped their hands.

"I'm feeling peckish," David said. "I'm going to try a mango." Tearing off a section of the skin, he bit into it. "Delicious—except that I'll spend the rest of the day getting the fibers out from between my teeth."

Eating a banana, Porter said, "I've only had one in my life before. It was good, but this one is first-rate!"

British West African currency was used here, but the soldiers found that their British currency was equivalent and desirable, so they were able to purchase samples of each kind of fruit, accompanied by much banter and laughter among the market women. Each time they concluded negotiations, an almost equal amount of fruit was added to the newspaper-wrapped bundle. "How generous they are," David commented.

Porter whispered, "We must have paid too much."

Meat of cattle, pigs, sheep and wild game was swarming with flies. Fresh fish glittered in the sun, and dried fish were displayed in abundance; huge smoked land snails from the forest formed dark brown mounds. Mingled with the squawking of chickens and guinea fowl were voices bargaining for every purchase.

Here among the fowl they asked for Dora Armar. Eager, smiling women pointed her out, amid shouts of "Dory, Dory, *bra!*"

"They are telling her, 'come,'" a woman told them.

She was short and fat, and her face seemed naturally to smile. Not just her mouth, David noticed, but her eyes and cheeks as well.

Dora Armar's English was quite good. "I'm so delighted, not just for this your letter for my husband. To know that you saw J. B., just two weeks past, you say?" She slapped her hands onto the front of her blouse in delight. "God be praised. He appeared well?"

David and Porter both assured her that her brother-in-law appeared to be healthy.

"I plan to go to my husband on Sunday next. He shall have the letter then." Dora folded the envelope and knotted it into a corner of her blue and yellow ankle-length cloth. She then opened the cloth slightly and wrapped it more firmly around her waist. David was so shocked that he didn't have time to politely look away before glimpsing a black slip. "You must come visit my farm. Just near Korle Lagoon, not far."

"Thank you, but we're leaving for Kumasi at noon today. There's no time."

Dora Armar wouldn't allow them to leave her without accepting a basket of several dozen eggs. "You no worry—they are hard-cooked," she said. "For the journey."

Amid smiles, shouted goodbyes and waves, the two men continued their exploration of the market. As one of them was tall and blond and the other had red hair, they attracted attention. But it was friendly attention, and they often heard the word *akwaba*.

The aromas of the market were as exciting as the sights and sounds. A rich banana smell drew David and Porter to an area where women were roasting plantain over charcoal fires. "Let's try it," said Porter.

"It's quite similar to banana," David said between bites. "But better, especially with these groundnuts she gave us. This, and all the fruit we've tasted, make a perfect breakfast."

Behind the food sellers sat an elderly tailor at a treadle sewing machine, making a pair of men's shorts. His broad smile revealed brown and rotting teeth. When he proudly held up the finished garment, Porter took some coins from his pocket. "How much?" he asked. The tailor held up one finger, and Porter said "One pound? He must be barmy!" Reaching out, the old man took one shilling from Porter's hand, holding it up to indicate that was the price. Porter said to David, "At that price, how can I lose?" and took the shorts.

"Porter, you don't even know if they fit you," David argued as they walked away.

"That's all right, old boy. They'll be a souvenir."

There were other men making dresses from colorful imported cloth. Now they all tried to sell their products to the soldiers. Porter and David pressed on, smiling and shaking their heads.

As they turned into another aisle of the market, they saw a crowd ahead and hurried to see what was going on. "There's a military policeman—no, two," David said.

Porter couldn't see over the bystanders. "What are they doing?"

"They seem to be taking a white man into custody. It's a British soldier, and he's resisting."

As the soldiers hauled their prisoner away, Porter asked what the man had done. The Africans in the crowd enthusiastically explained, all at one time, in their own languages. But David heard someone speaking English, and, looking down, discovered a boy dressed in the white shirt and khaki shorts of a schoolboy.

"The white man, he was urinating behind a market stall," the boy said.

"But we've seen many men urinating in public," David said.

"Yes, sah, but those are our Africa men. The *abrofo*, you whites, are not approving."

You speak English," Porter said to him. "Do you have time to show us around the rest of the market?"

"Oh, yes, sah. I would be most happy to."

The sound of hammers came from the carpenters' section. The din was so great that Porter and David were hurrying on when they caught sight of tiny chairs, tables, and beautifully crafted children's toys. "Do African children play with these?" David asked as he picked up a small locomotive.

"No, sah. They are for children of the *abrofo*." The child said.

He was very serious, and led the way to the next section, where second-hand European clothing was sold. David saw ladies' high button shoes, and long kid gloves. The customers were inspecting dresses of all kinds, but most of the garments were too small for many of the Gold Coast women, who tended to obesity.

"These clothings are called by us *obroni wawu*."

"But isn't that what children have been shouting at us?" David asked.

"Yes, sah. It translates 'white man is dead.' Africans are not believing that living people would give up their clothing in such good condition. The ignorant are thinking it comes only from those who have passed on."

"But why should they say 'white man is dead' when they see us?" Porter picked up a broad-brimmed lady's hat with ostrich feathers attached. As he placed it on his head in a comedic gesture, none of the women and children watching them seemed amused. David realized they must have assumed it was normal wear for men in England.

"It is the only words they know which contains *obroni*, or 'white man.' So they just shout the entire pair of words. Sah."

David noticed how late it was, and asked their guide to point the way to Christiansborg Castle. The boy insisted on walking with them until they were in sight of their destination. On the way, Porter asked how the youngster came to speak English so well. "I am studying English in school, sah. I am first in my class," he said proudly.

Porter asked, "What is your name?"

"I am named Francis Nkrumah, sah—but my birth name is Kwame."

"Well, Kwame Nkrumah, we must say goodbye. I hope we can be of help to you one day." Porter wrote their names on a slip of paper, and gave it to their guide along with a few shillings. "Please call on us if you need anything. We shall be with the Second Battalion, in Kumasi."

"*Medasi pi*, sah. That is meaning 'thank you very much.'"

As they walked on, Porter turned to see Kwame standing where they had left him, and waved. "He seems a pleasant chap. And bright, as well. Given half a chance, he should go far."

"How far can an African go in this world, no matter how bright he is?" countered David.

The two soldiers began preparing for the trip to Kumasi, and thought no more about young Kwame Nkrumah.

Chapter 9
Trek to Kumasi

The road from the coast to Kumasi was first cut by Ashanti warriors on their incursions into the coastal area for conquest, and later to deliver captives for the slave market. The distance was 125 miles, mostly through the rain forest.

David and Porter could ride in the trucks that carried the steel uniform boxes they had been issued at Christiansborg, as well as supplies, but the ride was so rough, they usually preferred to walk with the African soldiers. The going was easy enough along the coastal plain, but soon they climbed the escarpment to the forest. It was on the ascending road, with many switchbacks, that the two British officers were happiest to be walking. "On foot, I can enjoy this spectacular view of the Accra plain. If I were in one of those rocking, bumping vehicles on this narrow road, I'd be terrified," David confessed to his friend.

When they arrived at higher territory, they found huge trees, and the air was filled with the chirping and chattering of many birds. David was excited when he spied a gray parrot in the trees, and recognized the cawing of crows.

They came upon small villages and towns in forest clearings, and at Koforidua were surprised to see white people walking along the road and going into shops. When the troops were told they would spend the night there, David and Porter stopped at a Presbyterian mission, where the Scottish missionary warmly welcomed them for a meal and a bed for the night.

At dinner, David asked him about the large European presence in the town. "Our major Presbyterian settlements are up here on the Ridge; with our families, there are quite a few of us. Oh, there are missionaries near the sea, also," he explained. "There is a Basel Presbyterian Mission where you laddies are going, as well. It had to be rebuilt after the 1900 uprising, but I understand it's now quite impressive."

David did not mention that the Basel Mission was where his mother had grown up, and that he looked forward to seeing it.

The missionary passed the plate of roast pork to his guests. "We can raise our families here on the Ridge and not suffer the intense heat and humidity of the coast or the interior." He quickly added, "Of course, the Lord's work can be done anywhere."

That night, before they settled into comfortable beds, they each took a quinine tablet from their kits, the first of an evening ritual followed throughout their stay in Africa. "Lord, it's bitter!" David complained, trying to drown the taste with more water.

"But presumably it will save us from the dreaded malaria, old boy," Porter countered, as he did the same.

The next day, when they pushed deeper into the forest, the heat and humidity returned. When Porter complained, David told him, "You can always desert and settle on the Ridge, you know."

After some time, the wall of trees bordering the road began to depress David. He looked forward to the occasional village of thatch-roofed mud houses where the forest trees had been cleared.

At these villages, the trucks often had to wait while children chased the short-legged goats off the road. The inhabitants rushed out to smile and wave to the soldiers, who exchanged quips with them. David wished he could understand, and vowed to learn the language as quickly as possible. "Already know *akwaba*, and *medasi pi*," he told Porter.

"And remember *obroni wawu*."

"Not by a long chalk," David retorted. "I won't be dead for a long, long time."

The villagers offered water and sometimes food to the column, welcome supplements to the dried and tinned supplies they had brought along. David and Porter mentally thanked Dora Armar many times for her eggs.

At one village a young woman handed David and Porter gourd bowls of goat stew, and their mouths watered. After his first taste, Porter cried "Water, water!" The stew was hot with pepper. The young woman giggled as she produced a gourd of water; neither David nor Porter asked if it had been boiled. Alternately taking bites of stew and drinking water, they downed the food, and gave the woman a generous tip for her trouble.

In their tent that night, David asked Porter if he had noticed the young woman who had given them the food. "She was mighty good-looking, I'll tell you that," Porter answered.

"And how was she dressed?" David persisted.

"I don't know. Some kind of pretty cloth, I'd wager."

"Porter, she was wearing nothing above the waist. Her globes were right out there, round and shining. We've been here three days and you're so used to it you didn't notice?"

As he drifted off to sleep, Porter said, "I was paying more attention to the fire in my mouth, I guess."

Chapter 10
The Fort

It took them almost a week to reach Kumasi, and when they found their bunks in the Bachelor Officer Quarters, they both slept for a whole day.

When he awoke, David realized they were actually housed inside the Kumasi fort! As soon as he could find the time, he wrote a letter to Kate.

Dear Little Sister:

I'm in Kumasi at last. Arrived yesterday, and awoke today to discover my quarters (that I share with my pal Porter from Sandhurst) are actually inside the fort! Haven't looked around yet, but I can see it's huge.

We're bunked in the BOQ (Bachelor Officer Quarters to you), in one of the four corner lookout towers, from which we can see many houses with palm leaf roofs, and tall trees in the background. And tennis courts!

No screens on the big windows, but our cots have mosquito nets. This may be the place Father spoke of as his father's office.

We also look down on the inside courtyard of the place, where mother said the livestock were billeted. It's all military spit and polish now.

At our first meal Porter and I were asked if we played cricket or polo. So it's not all work here, any road.

Our kit includes six sets of Jaeger underwear! When I put those on, I feel like I'm living in luxury.

Cheerio!

Love,

Your far-flung soldier boy

It was good to have someone back home to whom he could write about this place. He knew he should be writing to his father, but decided to do that later.

As David and Porter met the other British officers billeted in the fort, the two friends agreed the situation here was much more relaxed than that at Sandhurst.

At dinner the first evening, David introduced himself to the lieutenant sitting next to him. "Doesn't the commanding officer take meals with us?" David asked.

"Oh, Colonel Taylor takes his meals in his quarters with his family, which is why things are so loud and bawdy here in the mess."

The soldiers, especially those who had been away from home for some time, often talked about their sweethearts back in England. Or about their African girlfriends here in Kumasi.

"Women seem to be a favorite topic of conversation, old boy," Porter observed one night early on.

David was falling asleep in his bunk. "Can you blame them? We have lots of conveniences here, but you have to agree there's a considerable lack of white women. And Colonel Taylor warned us about the local ladies, and what he called 'their loose ways.'"

Porter sat up in bed. "Yes, but he has a wife here. Have you met her? She looked awfully tense to me."

"Of course she's tense. It seems the colonel doesn't follow his own advice when it comes to local ladies."

Chapter 11
In the Forest

Second Lieutenant David Hodgson was heading for the forest with his squad of ten African recruits, most of them Hausas from the north. David's command of the Hausa language, which was the lingua franca here, was still rudimentary, though he and Porter studied every evening. "*Yi maci*," he ordered the men, showing off the little of the language he knew. To his surprise, the men marched forward as he had commanded. But he was glad the platoon sergeant spoke some English.

He was supposed to be teaching them the strategy of fighting among the trees, but knew he was learning at least as much as he taught them on the subject. The barefoot Africans stalked men as they had stalked animals all their lives: with silence and patience. In the dim light under the forest canopy, they could see the "enemy," who were other recruits from their own garrison, long before David could.

David had been surprised the first time he left the road and entered the forest; it was much darker than he expected, and, to his surprise, had very little undergrowth. The huge buttress roots of the kapok trees were strange barriers; it was like meeting a low wall. Even if the air on the road or path was scorching, inside the forest it was cool, and the air smelled of the rich earth. In the week he had been in Kumasi, David had grown to like the forest warfare exercises the best; he found pleasure in the dim coolness under the huge trees.

One day they came upon a cocoa farm. That's what his corporal called it, though it looked like no farm David had ever seen. That evening he sat at a table in the deserted mess hall, and by the light of a kerosene lamp, described it in a letter to Kate. "The cocoa trees were scrawny things, only about three meters high. They were growing right under the big forest trees! And hanging directly from the trunks and branches were these elliptical pods holding, I was told, the cocoa beans. Did you know that's where your morning chocolate comes from?"

The next day, David questioned the private who saw to his and Porter's needs, and was surprised to find him quite knowledgeable on the subject of cocoa.

"Sah, my father is being a cocoa farmer, and he say cocoa farming is only a small small time here in Ashanti. A man by the name Tetteh Quarshie secretly carry some cocoa beans here from another country. It no be difficult to be growing cocoa. Only small small plants under the big forest trees are having to be cut and cocoa planted there."

"How long a time before there's a crop?" David asked him.

"Five years only, sah."

Before they fell asleep that night, David told Porter of his discovery. "It's so easy to grow," he told his friend, "and there are such vast forests here in which to grow it. If the chocolate produced is high quality, cocoa could become a major export for the Gold Coast."

Several days later, David was again in the forest with his trainees when a scream startled him. He heard shouts of *kunama! kunama!* One of his recruits had stepped on a scorpion! And this was no ordinary small beige scorpion, like those David had seen preserved in the natural history museum in Lincoln. This one was almost a foot long, and dark brown. It lay dead near the little cluster of soldiers.

Otu, the injured soldier, was crying and babbling like a baby, holding his already swelling ankle. The other soldiers were crowded around him, offering sympathy and trying to help. The sergeant translated for David. "He say he be dying, sah, and the others dey say make he put mud on the wound, but he say offsah say what he go do."

"Is there a medical facility in this area?" David asked, not knowing if there was such a thing outside Kumasi.

"Yes, sah. Dey be dispensary at Asim, about fifteen minute march from dis place."

"What is this about mud on the wound?"

"Dat be our way, sah. Mud draw poison out."

"Do that quickly and then carry him to the dispensary, *yi maci!* quick march!" David ordered. They all hurried to follow his orders, and in ten minutes they were at the whitewashed building at the top of the hill.

Chapter 12
Scorpions Sting

David and the sergeant went to the window where Comfort registered patients. He saw that she was wearing a colorful blouse and skirt, and a bright cloth was wound around her hair.

"Do you speak English?" he asked the girl.

She looked at David's khaki West African Frontier Force uniform and then at his face. If the uniform had not prepared her, she would have been startled at the pale skin, as Dr. Findlay was the only white person who ever appeared at the clinic. "Yes, sir. What can I do for you? Are you ill?" As she said this, Comfort became alarmed. *Has my father ever treated a white man before? Does he know how to do it?* She scolded herself for such silly thoughts. She knew that, except for skin color, blacks and whites were physically the same.

"Oh, no. It's for one of my soldiers. He's been bitten by a scorpion."

"Stung."

"I beg your pardon?"

"Oh, I am so sorry." Comfort was embarrassed. "I spoke before thinking. But scorpions sting, not bite."

David demanded, "Tell the doctor he must be seen immediately!"

"Oh, yes, sir. I shall interrupt my father and ask him to see the soldier. He is not a doctor, but a dispenser. But he will know what to do—he is having many such cases." As Comfort spoke she left the window and went into the other room, and David looked around for the first time.

Waiting patients sat or lay on benches on the veranda. His soldiers were standing around their injured mate, who was lying on the cement floor. Otu's swollen ankle was now discolored.

David walked to the edge of the veranda and saw the town below him. Smoke from cooking fires rose among the palm-thatched roofs, and he could hear children laughing and singing. What a peaceful place to live, he thought.

Comfort soon came out to direct the group into a tidy white room. After the soldiers had deposited Otu onto the white cloth covering the wooden examining table, Comfort told them in Twi to wait outside. She spoke with such authority that the young men complied without even referring to David.

Kofi gave his attention to his patient and at first did not look at David. When he did, he was startled. David's pale blue eyes and fair lashes reminded him of Governor Hodgson's son. Kofi had seen him on the day of the governor's infamous speech—the speech that had led to the Ashanti uprising twenty-two years earlier. Kofi recovered his composure and spoke of the matter at hand.

In English, Kofi told David, "I see you have applied traditional medicine. Good—the poison is drawing out of the wound. I am now cleaning it with alcohol. I shall apply some more mud, but sterilized. Tomorrow you must be having the site cleaned again with alcohol. He will recover."

The scent of the alcohol stung David's nose. "Is there no Western treatment for scorpion bite—er, sting, sir?"

Kofi was startled. He had never been called "sir" by a white man. It gave him a feeling of power over this British soldier. "My experience has shown the traditional method being effective.

There are a number of local problems, such as this one, which you British have not encountered enough to be developing an antidote. In those cases, the traditional remedy may be the only remedy. In other cases, I am finding the traditional cure to be at least as effective as the Western one."

"For instance?" asked David.

"Such as boiling the stem and bark of a plant we call *mpatu-asa* for leprosy. Or using the leaves of *asaawa* for tropical ulcer." As he spoke, Kofi washed and disinfected the swollen ankle. "I saw both those complaints this morning. I gave the patients the Western remedy, because that is my duty. Sometimes I believe our traditional herbs are being more effective. In such cases, I suggest the patient to see an herbalist. In all fairness, I must say this: Many western treatments have wiped out diseases that were plaguing us Africans for centuries."

"It seems you think both African and Western medicine should be used?"

"Exactly." Kofi was flattered at the soldier's interest; he was enjoying this conversation. "But one great difference applies. Our traditional healers are never treating merely the affected part. They treat the whole patient. Other parts of the body may affect the diseased member. The mind is playing an important part in disease and in healing. African healers use this knowledge in their treatment."

"Would you explain to Otu what you are doing?" David asked. When the patient nodded eagerly to Kofi's brief vernacular explanation, the dispenser took some black mud from a pan and applied it to his ankle.

He turned to David. "Take this alcohol to use tomorrow, at the fort. You are coming from the fort in Kumasi, isn't it?"

"Yes, sir."

There it was again. Kofi almost liked this white boy, in spite of himself.

"Just be certain he is remaining calm and still for several days, and he will be fine. Have your men take him out to the veranda and let him rest there for a half hour whilst the poultice does its work. Then they may carry him to Kumasi."

Chapter 13
Conversations

While David waited on the veranda, he watched Comfort at work. She gently asked questions of each patient at the window, and recorded the answers on a card. She was a pretty girl, he noticed, with an attractive heart-shaped face. Her eyes, he thought, were a delicious chocolate brown color, as was her skin.

Comfort was dressed in a print cloth that had been made into a sleeveless blouse, with a similar piece wrapped around her waist and reaching to her ankles. David had noticed this when she ushered them into the examining room. He had also noticed her pleasing figure.

But she was too outspoken for an African. Imagine her correcting him, a British officer, regarding his error in calling Otu's wound a bite. But at least she had apologized, he thought.

When no more patients were at the window, David approached and spoke to her. "How is it you speak English so well?" he asked her.

"I am a secondary school graduate," Comfort answered proudly. She looked him in the eye as she said this, and David was impressed. He had thought all women in the Gold Coast were uneducated traders, or prostitutes. This one was quite different.

They chatted about her work at the clinic and her plan to become a nurse, and David told her of his job of training the recruits.

"But my real goal is to be helping my friends and neighbors here in Asim in some special way, and I haven't yet discovered how to do this," Comfort confided.

David couldn't make any suggestions, so he said, "Guess it's time to take our patient back to the fort!" He straightened his uniform jacket. "Thank you. Please give my thanks once again to your father for his kindness."

"You are quite welcome," she responded with a smile. David's knees weakened; never had he seen such a smile!

As another patient approached the window, David turned to leave. "Goodbye!"

"Goodbye, sir."

Later, David could remember nothing of the three-mile march back to Kumasi. After he had completed the necessary report of the day's incident and seen that Otu was comfortable, he lay on his bunk and visualized the face of the girl at the dispensary. He thought about their conversation on the veranda. He didn't even know her name!

Comfort, too, was thinking of the young soldier. She didn't speak to her father about him, as she knew how he hated whites. This omission bothered her. She had always confided to her father the things that were on her mind. She remembered how she had first seen the soldier's uniform, and then his face, with the off-center smile. And she remembered how concerned he had been for his injured soldier. She wondered how that blond hair felt to the touch, and was embarrassed at the thought.

Chapter 14
David is Banished

Two days had passed when Comfort again saw a khaki uniform at her dispensary window. She eagerly looked up, and her face brightened when she saw it was the young officer. "Good afternoon, sir. How are you keeping?"

"Good afternoon. I am fine, thank you. And you?" In his short time in Africa, he had learned that greetings were an important preamble to any conversation. One did not plunge headlong into one's business without honoring this formality.

"I am quite well. How is the soldier with the scorpion sting?"

David was thrilled that she remembered who he was. If he had known that he was the only British soldier Comfort had ever spoken to, he might not have been so impressed.

"Oh, he is recovering very well, thanks to your father's treatment."

"I am glad." Comfort wondered why the young man had come back, but was too well-mannered to ask. "May I invite you to come in and have some tea? I was just brewing it."

"I would like that, thank you." David watched as Comfort poured water from an enameled kettle into a flowered china teapot. "Where did you get the hot water?" The clinic did not appear to have running water, much less a cook stove.

"My cousin Yaw brings it to us from home every afternoon. I would prefer it to be hotter, but Yaw wraps it well and runs up the hill, so it makes acceptable tea."

"I don't see other Africans drinking tea. How do you come to be doing that?"

Comfort smiled. "My tutors at the Basel Mission School taught me more than academic subjects."

"You studied at the Basel Mission? So did my mother!" David was happy to have found a connection with this girl, who seemed intelligent as well as beautiful.

"Perhaps my father knew her, as he studied there also." Comfort's eyes brightened. "Were her parents missionaries?"

"Yes. Her father was headmaster of the school, a Reverend Ramseyer. They left . . ." David remembered that during the Ashanti uprising, escape from the besieged fort was the manner of his family's departure, and was embarrassed to go on. He sipped his tea, which was much too sweet. But it gave him something to do.

"During the 1900 war?" Comfort knew about this conflict. She had grown up on these stories, and now, here was a descendent of the enemy! "My father was fighting in that war. He has told me much about it. Did your mother talk about it with you?"

"Not much. My parents met in the fort when it was besieged, but I don't think they like talking about it." David had a thought. "Do you think your father would tell me about that war? I want to learn more about it. What my parents went through."

Comfort's expression changed. "Perhaps we had better not be troubling my father about that now. He is rather busy."

David gathered from the girl's demeanor that there was more to it than that. He handed Comfort the bottle in which Kofi had given him the alcohol, his excuse for coming back. As he did so, their hands touched. The contact was electric for them both.

"I will say goodbye, then, and thank you for the tea," David said, hating to leave. "But if I may, let me introduce myself. I am

Lieutenant David Hodgson. If you don't think me rude, I'd like to ask your name."

"Oh, no—not at all. I am called Comfort Akosua Mensah. Akosua is my birth name, and Comfort is my Christian name. Having an English name," she said proudly, "shows that I'm a Christian."

"You have a birth name?"

"Yes. It was determined by the fact that I was born on a Sunday."

"Does everyone in Ashanti have a birth name?"

"Oh, yes! For example, my father was Friday-born, so his name is Kofi. Kofi Mensah."

"But that means there are only seven names for boys and seven for girls!"

"True, but not everyone uses his birth name for everyday matters."

David was happy to find a subject for future conversation. "You'll have to tell me more about that, but not today," he said, glancing at the clock on the reception counter. Surprised at how late it was, he put down his drained teacup and stood.

"Goodbye, then," Comfort said, her voice reflecting her disappointment. Finding courage, she added, "I hope you visit again some time."

As Comfort and her father walked down the hill to Asim that evening, the air was growing cooler now that the sun was about to set, and the sky was bright orange in the west. Comfort asked, "Father, besides the governor and his wife, were there other European civilians in the fort when it was besieged?" Kofi didn't answer her question, but instead gave his reasons the Europeans should have died in the fort. He told her how disappointed he had been when so many escaped.

David visited the clinic several times a week after that, whenever he could get away. Twice, heavy rain forced him to cancel exercises with his men, and he had trudged the muddy road to Asim under an umbrella held by an African soldier.

He was puzzled that Comfort didn't seem to want him to talk to her father, who had been pleasant enough when they met.

On David's ninth visit to the clinic, Kofi came out of his office to find David chatting and drinking tea with his daughter.

"Good afternoon, sir." David stood. "I was in the neighborhood. I stopped in to pay my respects."

Kofi spoke sternly to him. "Good afternoon, sir. Thank you. Now, if you will excuse us, we have work to do."

As they walked home that evening, Kofi asked Comfort what the lieutenant wanted.

"Nothing, Father. He just likes to talk."

"And you?"

"Yes. I, too. He talks about things and places I have no knowledge of. He makes me feel there are many things in the world I have yet to learn about. He has come several times. I find myself looking forward to his visits."

Kofi was alarmed. "I forbid you to see him, and if he comes again you shall tell him that."

"But, Father! I cannot just tell him to go away!"

"That's exactly what you will tell him. I don't want any more discussion about it."

Several days later, when David appeared at her clinic window, Comfort told him what her father had said. She hated to do it, as she had enjoyed seeing him, and having their conversations, more than anything she had ever experienced.

However, Comfort was determined not to disobey her father, and David stepped away, turning to wave as he went down the path.

Her father sensed her sadness as they walked home. "Your soldier came again today."

"Yes, Father. I told him not to come back, as you said I should."

"Good. The Whites only know how to take from us. You'll not regret this, Comfort. You're better off."

"But Father!" Comfort tried to keep her voice from becoming a wail. "None of my friends here discuss other cultures, religions, and books. I did so enjoy our conversations!"

Kofi's jaw tightened. "You'll get over it."

Chapter 15
Unexpected Escort

David was frustrated at not being welcome to visit the clinic again. He had enjoyed his conversations with Comfort, and through them had begun to understand his Ashanti hosts. He knew that his fellow officers would have laughed at his referring to the Africans as their hosts, but David felt he was a guest in their country. He had learned much about Ashanti beliefs from Comfort, and about her tranquil life in Asim. Besides, she was a very attractive young woman; he wanted to see her again.

There were Sunday morning religious services at the fort, but this Sunday David attended services at the Basel Mission. He arrived early, and though the members of the congregation stared curiously at this unfamiliar British soldier standing outside, they nodded to him as they passed.

The Africans were dressed in their traditional finery: the men in colorful cloths and the women in bright cotton blouses and long wrapped skirts, with shawls to match. Their heads were wrapped in colorful head ties. The British also looked their best, the men in white suits and their wives in the clothes they had worn to church back home: long full dresses over tight corsets. He knew that women no longer wore such confining clothes back in England, but he had already learned that tradition dies hard in Africa. David guessed how uncomfortable these women must be; it was mid-morning and the heat hung over the town like a blanket. He was already sweating inside his woolen dress uniform.

By the time Comfort arrived with her friends Julia and Marie, the service was about to start. David stepped forward, offered his arm and quickly escorted Comfort into the church, leaving her companions staring in surprise. Comfort and David sat in the last pew.

"You should not have done that," she whispered. "People will talk!"

"But I had to see you!" he whispered back. "It's been two weeks, and I—I just needed to, that's all."

She smiled at him. "I am pleased." For the remainder of the service they avoided looking at each other, sitting far enough apart so their bodies did not touch.

Afterwards, most of the congregation stood outside, chatting. As soon as it was polite to do so, Comfort and David left the mission compound and walked toward Asim.

"Will you tell your father that we were together at church?"

"I will be surprised if he does not already know by the time I arrive home."

"What will he say?"

Comfort frowned. "I do not know. He forbad me to see you again, and I have disobeyed him. He will be very angry."

"Why doesn't he like me?" David was puzzled. "I got along well enough with him when we met."

"It is not you, in particular." Comfort took a handkerchief out of her cloth handbag and waved away a cloud of insects that seemed to follow them. "My father is having very definite ideas about white people in general."

"And what might those ideas be?"

Comfort took a deep breath. "That you belong in your country, and we belong in ours."

"So he thinks we should leave."

"Yes. He is quite determined about it."

"I'd like to discuss it with him, and give him our point of view."

Comfort was aghast. "I do not think that would be wise. My father does not allow a white person in the house, even Dr. Findlay."

They were nearing Asim, and David stopped in the shade of a neem tree and faced her. "Will you allow me to see you again?"

"Please do not ask me that now. I do not know." Comfort hid her face so he would not see her eyes.

When Comfort reached home, her father was waiting for her. He had, indeed, heard of the lieutenant escorting his daughter into church. Julia and Marie had arrived in Asim before her.

"Comfort, you know my wishes regarding this young man. Yet you have deliberately defied me. What have you to say?"

"Father, it wasn't like that. When we arrived at the church, there he was, and he just sort of swept me inside. I didn't want to make a scene."

"Did you wish to be 'swept inside' by this Englishman?" Kofi was trying to remain calm.

"Yes."

"Yes?" Kofi felt himself losing control.

"Father, the Englishman is my friend. And I enjoy his company. We like to talk." Comfort looked like she was about to cry.

"Do you realize the scandal you have probably already caused? African women who keep company with British soldiers are loose women, whom the soldiers only like because their own women are not here. Do you want the whole town thinking of you in that way?"

Now the tears were streaming down Comfort's cheeks. "I never thought of it like that. I don't care what people think or

say about me, but I never wanted to bring shame on you, Father."
Comfort set her Bible on her father's writing desk. "You are right.
I won't see him again."

"Thank you, daughter."

The following Sunday, David was again waiting outside the
church when Comfort arrived. She stopped long enough to tell
him she could not see him again, and went in to the service.

David was crestfallen. He knew the girl was fond of him and
that it was her father's orders she was following. He didn't go into
the church, but walked back to the fort and entered the room he
shared with Porter.

"I say, old boy, you're back early." Porter was a Freethinker,
and avoided religious ceremonies. He put down his book and took
off his glasses.

"I went, but I didn't go in. Remember I told you about this
swell African girl I met when Otu tangled with the scorpion? She
told me today that she could never see me again. I—I just can't
imagine that. Already I miss her!"

Holding his glasses up to the light from the window, Porter
carefully polished the lenses with his handkerchief. "Oh, she's just
leading you on. Playing hard to get, you know. She'll give in. Just
keep turning up and turning on the charm."

"Comfort wouldn't do that. She meant it." David felt more
depressed as he talked about it. "I know it was her father who made
her take that stand. He's probably worried about her reputation—
you know the kind of girls who usually associate with us."

Porter put on his spectacles and adjusted them in the mirror.
"Then you'll have to see her when nobody is around to gossip,
won't you?"

David's face brightened. "That's it! Oh, Porter, you are indeed
a man's best friend. Thank you!"

Chapter 16
Forbidden Trysts

The following Sunday morning David was again at the mission church. In his hand was a brochure about the Basel Mission and School that Comfort had given him. As she approached, David handed the leaflet to her with thanks. She nodded and continued into the church, and David walked away.

During the sermon, Comfort opened the brochure. There was a note! David begged her to meet him after church at the large termite mound along the Asim road. How could she do that, when she had promised her father? But, she thought, if nobody saw them together, then there would be no shame.

After church, Comfort and her friends were about to start home. "Oh, you two go on without me," Comfort told them. "I want to look in on Miss Mampong." She felt guilty, lying to her friends about visiting her former teacher, but didn't know how else to be alone on the road.

More lies would be necessary if she continued to see David, but she knew she couldn't stop now.

Giving her friends a head start, Comfort took the Asim road. When she came to the appointed place, she stopped and glanced up and down the road. Nobody was in sight. Not even David!

She was about to hurry on when she heard his voice from among the trees, calling her. She ran toward him, into the darkness of the forest. Before she knew what was happening, she was in David's arms. They held each other, and David kissed her gently on the lips. Comfort felt herself melting; she had never experienced such emotion! It was as if the entire world had disappeared, and all that remained was this wonderful man who was kissing her.

Without speaking, David led her to a space between the buttress roots of a kapok tree, where an army blanket lay on the ground. She sat down, and as he kissed her again, she lay back. David touched her face, and her hair, but when he put his hands on her body, she pushed them away.

"No! I cannot! Oh, please!"

David sat up. "You don't want me?"

"Yes, yes, I do. But it is wrong. I must wait until marriage..."

David bent over and kissed her again. "Oh, Comfort, I've longed for you so. When I thought I'd never be able to see you again, I realized how much I felt for you. Please."

Comfort reached up and ran her hand through David's hair, as she'd been wanting to do since the day they met. As she did, she knew they would be lovers; she had made the gesture.

David and Comfort met at this spot every few weeks after church. Comfort was afraid to invent a delaying errand too often, for fear her friends might become suspicious. When it rained, the lovers huddled under an overhanging tree branch as they talked.

One rainy day they watched flying ants emerge from their nests in the ground nearby. These were sausage-shaped insects, some as long as David's thumb.

"What in the world?" David asked when he first noticed them making their way out of the damp earth. As some flew at the lovers, David asked if they bit. Or stung.

Comfort laughed. "No, my darling. They do not bite or sting. They are just setting out in search of mates. Like all of us, I guess."

On fine days they made love, gently and sweetly. David was fascinated by the touch of Comfort's smooth dark skin, and Comfort loved the contrast of their bodies as he caressed her:

white against black. They both marveled at their good fortune in finding each other.

Afterwards, they discussed all that had happened since they last met. David had been promoted; he was now a captain. Comfort was very proud of him—but she regretted that she couldn't be proud of him in public.

One Sunday, Comfort spoke in what David thought of as her "purring voice." "I plan to leave in January for Nigeria for my training in nursing." David felt a great sadness at the thought of Comfort going away.

Comfort's happiness was clouded by her guilt at the web of lies she had created in order to have this time with David. She was no longer a carefree girl; she was a deceitful woman. Her life at home went on as usual: she walked to and from the clinic with her father and helped her mother at home. But she always carried the burden that she was hiding from them something they would never condone.

Chapter 17
Comfort's News

It was December. The last time the lovers met, they had seen a flock of large white birds fly over. Comfort explained, "Those birds, that you Europeans are calling cattle egrets, are a sign. They tell us that the harmattan, the dry season, is beginning. You will see." In the next few days, David noticed a dryness of his lips and skin. The wind had turned; no longer blowing from the ocean, it was now blowing from the Sahara Desert. The harmattan had indeed begun.

David waited eagerly for her every week. After three lonely Sundays he was relieved to see her approach their meeting place. As they embraced, Comfort said, "David, I must tell you something. Sit down."

They sat on a tree root. "Has your father found out about us?"

"No. I—I have not had my menses for three months. I am with child."

"Oh." At first, Comfort feared he was angry, but when he spoke, she knew she had misjudged him.

"Comfort, my love, will you marry me?"

Comfort put her arm around his waist. "You are very sweet and kind. But I do not want this to be the reason we marry. Let us wait, and see how we are feeling after the birth of the baby."

David kissed her cheeks. "When will the—when will you...?"

Comfort smiled. "When will I bring forth the baby? I think it will be May or June."

David held her close. "My darling—I'm so happy, and so sorry, both at the same time."

"Yes," Comfort whispered. "That is how I am feeling, too."

She told him she had to hurry home, but she had wanted to tell him about the child. She hurriedly kissed him and headed for Asim.

When David returned to the fort, he noticed the Christmas preparations. A decorated tree stood in a corner of the officers' mess, and he recognized a gramophone record that Kate had sent him, playing on the machine. Katie. He hadn't written her for months because he didn't want to tell her about Comfort and he didn't want to lie to her. He would have to write soon.

He found Porter involved in a game of drafts. "May I speak with you?" he asked his friend.

"Righto. I'm doing nothing but losing to this fellow, any road."

When they reached the privacy of their room, David threw his cap and jacket on his bunk while he told Porter that he intended to marry Comfort.

"Good God! You out of your mind? You can't! Don't you know that?"

"I'm determined to do it."

"But you must have the permission of the colonel. And I'll wager he won't give it to you. You'll get a lot of jiggery-pokery about regulations and such, but ultimately he'll say 'It's just not done.'"

"But she's pregnant with my child!"

"Oh, Lord. Now you have gone and made a mess, haven't you, old boy? Suppose the only thing you can do is help her out as much as you can. What sort of reaction has her family had to the news?"

"They don't know yet. Her father fought in the uprising of 1900 and hates all whites. What he'll say I have no idea." David had another thought. "He wouldn't throw her out, would he? We didn't even discuss that!"

"Well, I would suggest you do discuss it with her—before she breaks the news to her family."

Chapter 18
Change of Plans

The next day, David left his squad in Porter's charge and went to the clinic. Months had passed since he had been there, but it seemed like years. He was surprised to find the place looking much the same, except that the hibiscus were no longer in bloom and the jacaranda tree in front of the clinic was thick with flowers. The ground below it was covered with a lavender blanket of petals.

Comfort was writing in the patient log.

"David! What are you doing here?"

"I had to speak to you." David was breathless from hurrying up the hill. "Have you told your father yet?"

"No. I will wait a month or so, until it starts to show."

"I need to know what you think his reaction will be. I mean, might he make you leave?"

"Leave my home? Of course not! Oh, we are not so cruel as you English! He will be angry, but he will recover. The whole family will see that I am well cared for." She smiled up at David. "My—our baby will be as welcome as any other child."

Because she was pregnant, Comfort said, she could not go for nurses' training in Nigeria. "I shall have to wait a year to enter the next class," she said sadly.

"I'm sorry to hear that, but it means we won't be separated, so I'm not really sorry. "Oh, Comfort, I'm so selfish!"

"No, you're not selfish," she protested. "As for me, I, also, am happy to be seeing you in the coming months."

David smiled gratefully. "I'll be waiting for you by the termite mound. Please come next Sunday if you can."

"I will try. Now you had better be going, before Father finds you here. Goodbye." She touched her lips with her fingers, signaling a kiss.

Chapter 19
Outdooring

Comfort did not come until two Sundays later, explaining that her brother Kwaku's wife, Yaa, had given birth to a boy, and the outdooring ceremony had taken place the previous Sunday, early in the morning.

"Outdooring?"

"Yes. A newborn is kept indoors for the first eight days after birth, and a ceremony is held when the child is first outdoored."

"What did they name him?" David asked.

"Oh, he has many names. His birth name is Kwame, because he was born on a Saturday." Comfort sat down on the blanket David had spread. "But the birth name is not given; it is the soul's name that comes along with the baby at birth."

David was fascinated with Comfort's description. "Why wait eight days before naming him?"

"He really does have a name from the beginning, the day name he is born with. But we wait eight days to determine if the child really came to stay."

"Do some not stay?" David asked.

"Of course. Many babies are dying in that first week. We say they didn't like something here, such as the weather."

David noticed Comfort looked radiant, as if she were talking about her own child. "At the naming ceremony, we are giving other names, to show what greatness we expect of the child. His father has named him Addae, morning sun, because he was born at dawn. He should be a bringer of light all his life.

"We go through a ceremony to give the child certain characteristics, such as honesty, and each of us offers a name for the baby. And then we have a party!"

David nodded. "Of course, any excuse for a party!"

"He is such a beautiful baby, I cried when I held him."

"You cried? Because he was beautiful?"

"Perhaps I was thinking of our child and hoping he would be beautiful too, and aching to see him and hold him in my arms."

David put his arms around her. "I didn't even ask you—how are you feeling? Are you all right?"

"Oh, yes, my darling, I am feeling very well. Having your child inside me makes me happy all the time—even when I was a little sick upon arising. But I am past that, and am well."

David was relieved. "When do you propose telling your parents? Do you think I should be there?"

Comfort looked horrified. "Oh, no—that would make it worse! As for my mother, she will soon notice, as my European dresses have become tight. I now wear African dress all the time. The cloth only needs to be wrapped around me for the skirt. I plan to tell to them the news next Sunday, after our midday meal." Comfort giggled. "I just recalled a proverb of my grandmother: 'If you are in hiding, don't light a fire.' My belly will soon be my torch!"

"I feel guilty at not being with you when you tell them. Will they be upset?"

"My father will be angry when he learns that I am carrying your child. You know how he feels about Europeans. Now his grandchild will be half white. That will be difficult for him to accept. My mother will not cause problems; there are no longer any babies in the compound for her to care for."

David was not satisfied. "I want to speak to your father, and tell him I will take responsibility for the baby."

"That will not be necessary." Comfort smiled. "According to our custom, my brothers are the proper custodians of my child. Until they are able, my father will stand in for them. If he desires to see you, he will send for you."

Chapter 20
Telling the Family

The Mensah family ate their meals together, at a table in the courtyard. Kofi had insisted on this. At first, Afua was obviously uncomfortable, eating at a table, and with her husband. Traditionally, Kofi would have eaten before the rest of the family. But he was pleased to see that she had adjusted, and seemed now to be content with the arrangement. However, she never told other women that her family had such an unusual custom.

As the family were finishing their Sunday dinner, Afua got up to see to the kitchen. Afua's young nephew Yaw, who lived with the family and helped Afua around the house, had already cleared most of the remaining food and gone to feed it to the animals, and the children were at their schoolbooks while there still was plenty of natural light.

Comfort spoke to her parents. "I have something important to tell you." Afua sat down again.

"Please know that I do not want to hurt you, and am sorry if what I'm about to say is painful for you. I—I—"

"You are with child," Afua said.

Comfort nodded.

"What?" Kofi bellowed.

"Yes, father, I am pregnant."

"Who?" demanded Kofi, his eyes angry. He stood and loomed over his daughter.

"The British soldier who used to visit me at the clinic, David Hodgson. Father, we love each other." Comfort looked into her father's face.

"What did you say his name is?" Kofi demanded.

"David Hodgson."

Kofi overturned his chair. He howled, "Daughter, do you realize who this man is? He is a descendent of the man who prompted us to go to war in 1900!" Kofi's fist hit the wooden table and crumbs jumped into the air. "Not just a white man, but of the family of our enemy! Don't you know it was a Hodgson whose actions brought about the deaths of so many Ashantis?"

At this Comfort began to cry, and Afua begged her husband to be silent.

Kofi shook his finger at his wife. "Why haven't you taught your daughter about men? That is your responsibility, and it is clear you have not fulfilled it."

Kofi stomped around the courtyard. He raised his arms to the ancestors. "What kind of daughter have you sent me?" To Comfort, who was sobbing with her head in her mother's lap, he shouted, "What did they teach you at the mission?"

Kofi lifted the cloth he was wearing to wipe the sweat from his face and neck, and his eyes were wild and red. "Oh, my daughter, how could you do this? When people see the child has white blood, they will think you are a woman who goes with the soldiers for money." Kofi's voice was filled with despair.

"But he wants to marry me," Comfort wailed into her mother's breast. "I told him to wait until I give birth, and then we would consider it."

"Marry him! That would be worse! Comfort, I told you not to see him again and you disobeyed me. You disobeyed me! You see what that has led to. Now I tell you again—you are not to see him ever again. Is that understood?"

Comfort sat up in her chair. "Yes, Father, I understand you." She swallowed and spoke in a firm voice. "But I cannot obey you. Forgive me, but seeing him will get me through this pregnancy and the disgrace that will follow. Please understand."

"I'm trying to understand you. I cannot lock you in the house. You know my feelings about this. I will discuss it no more." At this, Kofi strode from the courtyard.

Afua spoke as she stroked her daughter's hair. "Are you feeling all right?"

"Oh, yes, mother, I feel fine. My morning illnesses have passed."

"I know. I could see that you were not well in the mornings, but was waiting for you to tell me yourself. It will be good to have a baby in the compound again."

"Oh, thank you, mother!"

"But you were a foolish girl to let that soldier take advantage of you. Have I taught you nothing?"

"He didn't 'take advantage' of me. I told you, we love each other."

"A European? He may even have a wife and children at home. In any case, he'll go back to England and you'll never hear from him again."

A week later, Comfort repeated this conversation to David as they lay on the blanket under the kapok tree. "Neither of them can accept that a white person and an African might be finding each other attractive. But to my mother, the important thing is the child." Comfort smiled. "I know she looks forward to helping me raise it. Already she advises to me about my pregnancy, and what I should avoid eating, and how to have a healthy child."

"Helping you raise it?" That phrase stuck in David's mind. "I thought we would raise our child together!"

Comfort touched David's hair. "My dear, you know that is impossible. You will go on with your army career. Your offspring will be living here, with me and my family. You may visit the child whenever you like. Perhaps when he grows older, he will come to you in England."

David was dumfounded that Comfort had thought this all out, and had made a unilateral decision. He knew it was the only solution, but he didn't want to admit it. David felt emasculated by his helplessness in this situation. "Let's talk about it again, later."

Chapter 21
The Reverend's Reaction

Much more severe than her father's reaction was the response of Reverend Boerne at the Basel Mission Church. Comfort had gone to the German missionary's office to ask his advice about her situation and her relationship with David. She got no advice from him.

"You're pregnant!" He shouted from behind his heavy wooden desk as soon as she told him the news. "Comfort, you were a model student. Since graduation you've been so faithful to the church—and now this! And with a British soldier! The church cannot have such poor examples when we are trying so hard to recruit new members!"

Comfort stared, open-mouthed, as the red-faced pastor raved.

"Comfort, I do not want you seen in church in your condition. You must stay away until after you give birth. Then I will allow you to return."

"But Reverend..."

"No argument! You are fortunate I have not removed you from the church rolls for your sin."

Comfort made a quick decision and responded. "You may remove me, Reverend. You will never see me here again. And I am no longer using the Christian name, Comfort, that you gave me when I was baptized. I am Akosua Mensah."

Comfort had been taught that the reverend was the closest person to God. She did not argue, or even become angry. For the first time since she realized she was pregnant, she was ashamed. She rose from the rickety chair and left the room with a "Thank you, Reverend." She never entered a church again.

After her conversation with Reverend Boerne, Comfort Mensah was no more. She told her friends and family she would only answer to Akosua.

Chapter 22
Smallpox!

"Oh, David! A tragedy!" Akosua and David had again met in their secret place after several weeks of David waiting in vain for Akosua to turn up.

"Akosua! Is the baby all right?"

"Oh, yes, darling. But my brother, Kwaku, who I told you has just fathered a child? He's dead!"

"Dead? Did he have an accident?"

"No! He had what my father said was smallpox!" Tears ran down Akosua's cheeks as she explained. "And now his child is fatherless, although his wife's brothers will see to the baby's needs."

"You're certain of that?" David looked skeptical.

"Oh, yes." Akosua nodded. "Traditionally, we are considering the brothers of a child's mother are actually closer relations to the child than is the child's father, as there is a clear blood tie. So they are the ones responsible for the child."

"And your brother died of smallpox?"

"Yes" Akosua dried her tears on a corner of the cloth she was wearing. "Father says there is an epidemic of smallpox to the east of us, in the French colony of Cote d'Ivoire, what you call the Ivory Coast. And Kwaku traveled there several weeks ago to visit a cousin—we didn't know of the epidemic."

"Was he ill when he arrived home?"

"Yes, his body hot with fever, and at first we thought it was malaria. But father said it was this smallpox, and made Kwaku to be staying away from everyone else. 'Isolation,' Father called it. By the time the pox started to appear, my poor brother was very ill, and he soon died. We are hoping that no person caught the disease from Kwaku."

"Is there no cure for smallpox?" David had never known of a case, as in England, compulsory vaccination had been in place for many years.

"Father says there is not; only vaccination before one is exposed to the disease."

Chapter 23
Farewell in the Forest

In the following months, David and Akosua continued to meet occasionally. As her belly swelled, Akosua found it less convenient to come to their meeting place. She pretended to go to church every Sunday morning, and sometimes met him as if she were coming from there; she had not told anyone that she had been forbidden to attend.

David discovered, to his surprise, that his sexual desire for Akosua, which only months before had overwhelmed him, was dwindling. He told her he was afraid of hurting the baby, and she accepted his explanation without protest.

They were lying on their blanket, holding each other and listening to a bird in the tree above them. "Coo—coo—coo-coo-coocoocoocoo," it lamented. David pointed, and they saw the pink underbelly of a wood dove, and flashes of dark blue as it flew from branch to branch. Akosua whispered, so as not to disturb it.

"I shall not be coming here again. My condition..." She couldn't finish, and turned to sob into David's chest. Akosua knew it wasn't her condition, but the fact that seeing David was not so important to her any more. She had transferred her devotion to the baby.

David saw Akosua falling into the welcoming arms of her culture. She was too comfortable there to change. There would be no marriage and he would not raise his own child. He felt a great despair at this, but knew he could not fight the influence of this close-knit African society. The lovers kissed and embraced for the last time under their tree.

Akosua told him, "I shall send word to you when the baby is born, so you may come see it. Goodbye, David."

"Wait!" He reached under a corner of the blanket and brought out a small framed painting. "My sister Kate painted this. Will you take it, so my child can grow up knowing what his father looks like?"

This was the first indication that David had accepted her declaration that he would not help raise the child. Akosua was relieved and saddened at the same time. "Of course. I will treasure it. As will your child."

Chapter 24
Bad News

About a month later, David's friend Porter appeared at the clinic. Akosua saw the uniform before she looked up at his face. As she raised her head, her disappointment showed, and Porter started by apologizing. "I'm sorry I'm not David, miss. I know who you are, as he described you to me. My name is Lieutenant Porter Damon, and I'm David's best friend here. We shared a room in the officer's quarters."

"Shared a room? You no longer do?" Akosua became apprehensive. She felt her baby react with a kick, and she winced. "Come in, please, and have a seat. What do you want to tell me?"

"It's David, Miss. Just a week ago he developed a fever. He took quinine for it, but it just got worse. They put him in the post hospital, where he was delirious most of the time. But he made me promise to tell you if anything happened to him." Porter hesitated. "That's why I'm here. This morning he—he died. I'm very sorry."

Akosua sat, silent, trying to take in what Porter had told her. He died. He's dead. My baby's father is dead.

David is dead.

There was a silence while Akosua sat, unable to speak. A waiting patient groaned, and weaver birds chirped in the jacaranda tree.

When she nodded her head, Porter said goodbye and hurried down the hill.

Akosua rose from her chair at the window and walked into her father's examining room. A patient was with him, and he looked up at his daughter with annoyance—until he saw her face.

"What is it?"

"Father, I am not well. Please allow me to go home now."

"Yes, if you feel that's best."

"Thank you, Father. There are only three patients waiting, and I have made out cards for each of them."

"Your mother will see to you. You need help walking down the hill?" Kofi rose to his feet, but Akosua shook her head, and he sat down again. "Good. Be well, Akosua."

That evening, after she had rested, Akosua told her parents what the soldier had said. Afua cried, but Kofi remained stern-faced. "It is truly our own child, now," he said.

Yes, thought Akosua, it is truly my own child. She realized she had thought of it that way the last time she had seen David, and felt guilty.

Porter Damon came to the clinic one more time, to tell Akosua he had written to David's parents about the child.

"Oh, thank you. Have they replied?"

Porter hesitated, looking at the floor. "David's mother answered my letter. She said she knew of such schemes for getting money from the families of deceased soldiers, and didn't want any part of it."

At dinner that evening, Akosua told her parents what David's mother had said.

"Do you know anything about his family?" Kofi asked.

Akosua told them everything she knew about David. When she informed them that David's parents had met in the fort during the siege of 1900, and that his maternal grandfather had been head of the Basel Mission, Kofi struck the table with his hand—the same table he had struck when learning of Akosua's pregnancy.

"My classmate Trudi Ramseyer—the child's grandmother!"

Afua was excited. "Then you must write to her about her grandchild!"

Kofi thought a moment. "No. Lieutenant Damon has written and she has refused to be involved. Leave it at that."

Chapter 25
Akosua's Baby

It was an easy birth, with Afua and the village midwife in attendance. Akosua knew it was a natural process, and was not anxious about it.

The child was a fair-skinned boy. Akosua was excited when she saw his blue eyes, but, as Afua had predicted, they darkened after a few months. They became a hazel color, with yellow glints. His sand-colored hair was curly.

The unnamed baby was kept indoors until eight days after birth. On that day, his naming ceremony was held, beginning before sunrise.

The father has the responsibility of naming the child, and Porter Damon stood in for David, though everyone knew that a child inherits his father's soul, or *ntoro*, even if the father is deceased. The baby's *mogya*, his flesh and blood, come directly from his mother.

A village elder poured a libation of local gin on the ground, asking the divinities and ancestral spirits to assist with the proper naming of the child.

"Now you are naming him, Porter," Akosua urged.

Porter held the boy in his arms and named him Joshua (a strong man) Adjei (messenger from God) Hodgson. Kofi had reluctantly agreed that his grandson should bear his father's surname. Of course, since Joshua was born on a Sunday, his birth name was Kwasi.

An elder dipped his finger into a cup of water and touched it to baby Joshua's lips, saying, "When you say it is water, it is water." The elder dipped his finger into a cup of gin and placed it on Joshua's mouth, saying, "When you say it is strong drink, it is strong drink."

Akosua explained to Porter and to Dr. Findlay, whom Akosua had invited, "This is showing him the necessity of always living in harmony with the truth for all of his life."

The guests presented gifts for young Joshua, and the bottle of gin was shared with them as the elder repeated the baby's full name to each guest, who then added another name. Akosua explained, "Each person sipping the gin is showing his or her respect for my baby, and wishing him good health.

"His names are expressing the function for which the Supreme Being has conceived Joshua and for which the Earth Mother has borne him."

"And what is that function?" Porter asked, carefully returning Joshua to his mother's arms.

"That remains to be seen," Akosua replied.

Chapter 26
Back to the Clinic

After the outdooring, Akosua stayed home with her baby. He slept most of the time, especially after a meal at his mother's breast. Afua was delighted to have a baby in the house, and tried to discourage her daughter from going back to work, as she knew young Joshua would be going with her.

Kofi had made a small bed for the baby, using a strong cardboard box in which some of the clinic supplies had been sent. He tucked in some soft white cotton cloth from England, part of the supply he used at the clinic. This made a perfect bed for Joshua, who occasionally used it during the day. At night, he slept with his mother.

Kofi said he liked doing things for his grandchild. At home, he would hold the baby on his lap and play with him untiringly, making him laugh. He often sang a children's song to Joshua in the Twi language, *"Tue Tue Barima."* "Sorry Man, Sorry/ This small boy/ Has made you fall flat/ Sorry, sorry." At the line "Has made you fall flat," Kofi would fall back suddenly. No matter how often he did this, Joshua would unfailingly laugh delightedly. Kofi commented that this also gave him some much-needed exercise.

But Akosua was concerned that her father was running the clinic alone. When she asked him how he was managing, he always replied with an Ashanti proverb, one of many he'd learned as a child from his adopted mother. One of Kofi's favorites was, "The moon moves slowly, but it crosses the town." But she understood that he could spend less time treating his patients, as he had to register them as well as order and unpack supplies, update the inventory and wash the glassware.

So it was only a few weeks before Akosua announced that she would go back to work the next day. Afua resisted, but her daughter was adamant. Kofi, on the other hand, was delighted.

With Joshua on her back, she walked up the hill with her father. "We're fortunate that your grandson does not cry much," she said that first morning. He was, in fact, sleeping on her back as they climbed.

The routine at the clinic was only slightly affected by the baby's presence. He was on Akosua's back most of the day, but when he became restless, she knew he was hungry, and she put him on her lap, lowered her cloth, and breastfed him. Patients who came to the window could see the baby suckling, and would sometimes comment on the joys of motherhood. She had a supply of clean cloths that she wrapped around his bottom for diapers, and each afternoon she carried home several soiled ones, which she washed the next morning before going to work. They dried in the sun much of the day; Kofi said that was a good way to sterilize them.

While the three of them were at home for lunch, Joshua slept in his little bed, but he seemed happy to be put on his mother's back again for the afternoon.

Akosua never tired of caring for her son. He was all she had of his father, and each time she looked at his face she saw David. She wondered if she could bear to be without her child while she went through the nurses' training course.

Chapter 27
A New Project

As Akosua worked at the clinic, she often thought about the smallpox epidemic to the west. She wondered if it were possible to prevent the epidemic from harming her family, and she decided to discuss it with the Colonial Medical Officer when he next visited the clinic.

Dr. Findlay unexpectedly appeared one morning, and Akosua could see him blushing when he saw Joshua nursing at her breast; she quickly laid a cloth lightly over her baby. Dr. Findlay had been in the Gold Coast long enough to know the Africans did not hide their breasts and nursed their babies in public, but he appeared uncomfortable anyway.

Akosua told the doctor, "I'd like to discuss with you what I might do to help if the smallpox epidemic spreads to Kumasi and Asim. You may be knowing that my brother died from the disease, so it is a concern of mine."

"Actually, there is something that should be done before the disease spreads to this area." Dr. Findlay had come into the small registration room and sat on a chair facing Akosua. "And I think you might be a good candidate to participate."

Akosua's eyes brightened.

Dr. Findlay continued, "You probably are unaware of the fact that inoculation against smallpox was mandated in 1920 for all residents of the Gold Coast Colony."

"What means this 'mandated'"? Akosua asked.

"It has been ruled that it must be done."

As she discreetly moved Joshua to her other breast, Akosua asked, "And has it been done?"

Dr. Findlay did not look at the suckling baby. "It has in the original colony, along the coast. But in the Ashanti region, it has not been done, mainly because we don't have enough staff. But with the epidemic in Ivory Coast, I think we should try to do it now."

Dr. Findlay saw Akosua's eyes widen. "Might you be willing to help with this? I've seen you work with patients at this clinic, and I think you may be a good candidate."

"What would I be doing?"

"You'd be vaccinating people against smallpox."

Akosua's brow furrowed. "But I'm not a nurse! Would people be allowing me to do this?"

"I think they will. You're known here in Asim, and carrying Joshua on your back will make you more acceptable to strangers."

"And what of father and this clinic?"

"Oh, we'll find someone to take your place here," the doctor said. "You probably know someone who would like to do it."

"Yes, several of my friends have questioned me about employment at the clinic." Akosua shook her head. "But I was meaning why would father not be doing this vaccinating here at the clinic?"

"Oh, he would do it as well, to those who come to the clinic."

"So those patients might be getting two vaccinatings."

"He would mark with gentian violet dye the wrist of those he vaccinates, as would you mark those to whom you give the inoculation, so nobody gets it twice." The day was growing warm, and Dr. Findlay wiped his brow with his white handkerchief. As always when visiting the clinic, he wore a suit.

"Excuse me, doctor. Would you like to remove your jacket? You must be very warm."

"That's very kind of you, Akosua, but I'll keep it on. I think of it as my uniform, and I'll only remove it to put on my white coat when I look in on your father." The doctor smiled at her. "And you would wear a white coat when you do this vaccinating, to show that you are a health worker."

The idea of wearing a white coat, like a doctor, appealed to Akosua, and she became even more interested in the whole idea. "But I've never injected anyone, and don't know how."

Findlay smiled. "Smallpox vaccination is not an injection, Akosua. You simply scratch the skin in a small area and apply the vaccine to the broken skin.

"The vaccine is made from a similar virus, called 'cowpox,' so the vaccination cannot cause smallpox, and only provides protection."

"Does the person then become ill with this cowpox?"

Dr. Findlay shook his head. "Very few people do, and it's not a serious disease."

Akosua became more excited about the job. "Oh, Dr. Findlay, I'm very much interested in doing this. I might be saving people's lives!"

Dr. Findley smiled and nodded. "That's true, Akosua."

As Joshua seemed no longer hungry, Akosua stood, moved him under her arm to his usual place on her back, and re-tied the cloth that was holding him. She then placed a large cloth over him and secured it with a twist over her breasts.

"I think you should be discussing this with Father, before I become too much excited about it. His patient has just left, so he'll soon be coming out."

Just then, Kofi appeared, and Akosua hurried off to bring another chair.

Kofi stopped in the doorway when he saw the visitor. "Dr. Findlay! I didn't know you were here. Has my daughter offered you some tea?"

"Oh, Father, Yaw has not yet brought the hot water." Akosua entered the room, carrying a wooden stool.

"No worry, Kofi. I don't need any tea, as long as I might have some of your boiled water to drink."

Akosua put down the stool and left the room.

"Good to see you again Kofi," Dr. Findlay remarked.

Kofi smiled. "I've aged a bit since you were last seeing me here. In the old days, when I was a new dispenser, we met often. You were a great helper in explaining to me this your white man's medicine."

"And you to me also, Kofi. I learned much from you about African methods of treating diseases."

Akosua returned with a gourd of water. "Here you are, doctor." Sitting silently on the stool, she listened while the doctor explained the smallpox vaccination project to her father. Kofi nodded periodically, and asked several questions. When Dr. Findlay was finished, Kofi asked Akosua how she felt about the project.

"Father, I think it's a good thing to be doing, and we would be saving lives if the epidemic were to be coming here."

The doctor smiled at Akosua's enthusiasm. "I shall return tomorrow with the vaccine and show you both how to administer it to your patients. Please have several oranges available, as you can practice with them, and then I'll ask you to vaccinate each other."

Chapter 28
Rehearsal

Two weeks later, after a local woman had been trained to take Akosua's place at the clinic and both Kofi and his daughter felt confident in vaccinating, the project began.

After dinner the day before she was to begin vaccinating, Akosua described to her parents in the Twi language what her day would be like. Her younger brothers came one by one to listen to her portrayal, and Yaw had left his dishwashing and was standing nearby.

"In my white coat, I stand outside the doorway of a house with Joshua on my back and Abena, the village youngster I recruited to carry my bag of equipment. I shout 'Kaw, kaw, kaw.'" Akosua knocked on the wooden table. "Generally, people will know me as a neighbor, and clearly a mother, so they'll be happy to see me.

"'Akosua, you are welcome. Come in! Have a seat, please.'" Akosua used a higher pitched voice for the other people in her story, which made her brothers giggle. "As I sit down, my host usually will offer me water to drink, as custom dictates."

Her father interrupted. "Akosua! You won't drink it, will you?"

"Not unless I know that this family boiled their water," she replied. "I might accept the water but not drink it. I would then ask after the health of members of the family, and write in my record book if any of them were ill or away from the house, so I can return to inoculate them."

Akosua pulled from her bag her record book with its mottled black-and-white covers. "That looks just like my exercise book for school!" young Yaw interrupted.

"Yes, it's the same kind of book. I will have a page for every family, and Dr. Findlay has provided me with more books."

She went on with her description. "'I'm here to give everyone in the house a vaccination to prevent smallpox,' I say, 'except babies less than a year old.'" Akosua was practicing her procedure as she told it to her parents.

"I show them the two-pronged metal needles I use." Akosua showed her parents one of the tools the doctor had provided.

"You call this a needle?" her oldest brother, Kwaku, asked. Akosua had used the English word, needle.

"It doesn't get pushed into the flesh like a hypodermic needle, but you know it's sharp," she told him.

She resumed her role-playing. "'I'll scratch the skin in a small area of your upper arm and put a drop of the vaccine on it.' I assure them that the small amount of bleeding that might occur is normal.

"'You'll have a red, itchy bump there in a few days, which will become a blister that eventually dries up. In about three weeks the scab will fall off and you'll have a small scar. And you will not catch the smallpox.'" Akosua recited this, as she had said it to herself so many times.

"You both have gone through this when I vaccinated you," she told her parents. "And when Father did you boys." Her parents nodded.

"My host will listen carefully, and maybe the family will gather around her. The younger children might react when I mention the blister," Akosua says with a smile. "Someone might ask what it means if that blister doesn't appear, and that will show me they're listening."

"'That means your vaccination wasn't successful, and the vaccine I used didn't go into your body as it should,' I tell them." Akosua now looked very serious. "I say it's very important that they let me know of this, and I shall come and vaccinate them again.

"Oh, I almost forgot. If a person says he already was vaccinated by you, Father, I check his wrist for your bluish-green stain. And after I vaccinate someone, I dab some gentian violet on the person's left wrist."

"Can people refuse to let you do it?" Kwaku asked.

"Most of the village residents know and trust me, and they accept the notion of being protected from the deadly smallpox by the vaccination. I don't think I'll have any difficulty.

"And I tell the children that their reward for getting vaccinated would be their very own pencil."

Afua spoke for the first time. "A pencil? Who pays for those? Not you, I hope!"

Akosua laughed. "Oh, no! I suggested to Dr. Findlay that he ask the chief of Ashanti to donate them, and to everyone's surprise, the Asantehene agreed!"

"You seem to be enjoying the prospect of this work of yours," Afua said.

"Oh, I am! I'll like seeing the neighbors I know, and meeting the few I didn't know. And to realize that I'm actually saving people's lives makes it the best possible job!"

Chapter 29
A Thorn in the Campaign

Auntie Nana was an elderly childless widow living alone in a small hut on the outskirts of Asim. Generally bad-tempered, she had few friends. But because of her age, many people respected her opinions. When she heard of the vaccination project, she told anyone who would listen about her experience as a child. "I had a vaccination from arm to arm when I was young. They scratched my arm until the blood came, then they rubbed in blood from someone who had the smallpox. It all swelled up, but it healed, and I never got the disease. That's our traditional way."

Auntie Nana did not trust the modern method of scratching the skin and using a medicine, as she called it. "It's the white man's way of poisoning us."

She warned everyone against Akosua and her vaccinations. Most people did not trust Auntie Nana's opinion about being poisoned by the *abrofo*, but there were some who thought there might be some truth in what she said, and complained to others about it.

As a result, a number of villagers refused to be vaccinated, saying only that they didn't trust the white man's medicine. Though disappointed, Akosua could do nothing about them.

Almost all villagers had heard of Auntie Nana's resistance, and many were not as readily accepting of vaccination as Akosua had hoped. She spent much of her time assuring people that it would protect them against the disease, and that cowpox, in the rare event that it should develop, was a very mild disease.

When she came home in the evening, Akosua was often very tired. "I had no idea this would be such hard work," she complained to her mother. "I never realized I'd have to make so many return visits to a family, as the mother was at the market, or the father was with another wife, and I'd have to be sure and chase them down.

"Joshua doesn't like the long hours, either, which is why I sometimes send the girl Abena to you with the baby when he becomes fussy."

"Do you think he might be fussy because you're not as calm and happy as you used to be? Your milk is probably not flowing as well as it was, either." Afua had often been able to put her finger on whatever was troubling a small child.

Akosua realized the truth in what her mother suggested, and determined not to allow frustration to affect her enthusiasm for the job. After maintaining a positive attitude and cheerful demeanor, she soon saw Joshua becoming more calm as well.

Chapter 30
The Vaccination Project

For the next several months, Akosua and her young helper could be seen daily in Asim, going from house to house to vaccinate residents. She soon realized that keeping careful records was key.

At one house early on, an elderly woman told her of the arm-to-arm vaccination she had received as a child. "It seemed to protect some, but others used to die; your way of doing it is better."

When Akosua related this to Dr. Findlay, he shook his head. "In fact, this practice became a problem for colonial medical campaigns, because in providing protection for most people, it also spread the disease."

Some children were at school, and that required a return visit to the house. Akosua was determined to overcome at least this obstacle.

At the newly opened elementary school in Asim, Akosua convinced the head teacher to allow the children to be vaccinated there. The gentian violet wrist stain and careful record-keeping were crucial to her work, and Akosua was fastidious about both. And the children were delighted with their very own pencils.

She was heartened by the eagerness of most people to get protection from the dread disease, and the assurance that they would let her know if a blister had not formed.

After several months, when almost everyone in Asim had been vaccinated either by Akosua or her father, the project extended into Kumasi. Akosua was able to vaccinate many residents before the epidemic emerged there, at which time Dr. Findlay decided she shouldn't continue.

"Congratulations, Akosua!" Dr. Findlay was smiling as Akosua entered his office in Kumasi after the epidemic had declined, and no new smallpox cases had been reported for two weeks.

"Congratulations? I am so disappointed that I could not save the Kumasi people who have died."

"But all those 122 people, as well as the few who caught the disease and survived, lived in the part of Kumasi you didn't vaccinate, and absolutely nobody in Asim has contracted the disease. There was one death in Kumasi of an Asim woman who had recently moved there. It appeared she had not been vaccinated."

On hearing the deceased woman's name, Akosua realized that she was one of the few who had refused vaccination. She decided to inform Auntie Nana of the woman's death.

Aunti Nana sobbed when Akosua told her. "That woman was a neighbor of mine," she said softly. "I feel so guilty; I am responsible for her death."

Akosua gave her the names of the others who had refused vaccination, and suggested that Auntie Nana convince them to go immediately to Kofi's clinic to have it done. Several weeks later, Akosua was pleased to learn that all had been vaccinated.

Doctor Findlay was pleased as well. "Now you have a one hundred percent vaccination record in Asim! If you want to go for nurses' training, you still have time to register."

Grinning, Akosua said, "I am so happy at saving so many people's lives. But if it is acceptable to you, I'd like to stay and be vaccinating the remaining people in Kumasi. I'm thinking that's more urgent than being trained in nursing," she said. "I must confess I am finding this work very satisfying."

Doctor Findlay smiled. "Akosua, that is very generous of you, and we shall arrange it."

Chapter 31
Celebration!

Gratitude was on the mind of the Asimhene, the chief of Asim. He puzzled for several days over what he could do for the young woman who had saved his village from the scourge of smallpox.

Finally, he convened the Traditional Council for suggestions. One member had a relative in Kumasi who had died of smallpox, and he suggested a durbar be held in Akosua's honor.

"But durbars are usually held for such purposes as honoring an ancestor or calling upon the deities for prosperity and unity," the Asimhene said.

"Can we not hold a durbar to thank the ancestors and deities for sending this young woman to protect us?" another council member asked. This was acceptable to the entire group, and plans were begun for the celebration.

A member of the council was appointed to visit Akosua and her family to inform them of their decision. When she was told of it, Akosua immediately said, "No, I don't deserve anything like this." She was embarrassed at the thought.

"But the Asimhene has appointed me to let you know we plan to do this! I can't go back to him and say you refuse!"

Akosua realized she had no choice in the matter. "Please tell the chief I'll be honored."

The chosen site was the sports field at the new Asim elementary school. Everyone in the village was invited to attend, as well as the chiefs and their retinues from surrounding towns and villages, Dr. Findlay, and drumming and dancing groups from the region. Akosua sent a message to David's friend Porter, inviting him to come.

On the appointed day, hundreds of visitors arrived in Asim, and by early afternoon the hastily built bleachers were crowded with spectators, and as many people were standing. The chief of Asim arrived, and he and his wife were seated in upholstered chairs in front of the bleachers. Akosua and her parents were seated behind them in the first row. Joshua, now more than a year old, was on Akosua's lap, and Dr. Findlay and Porter sat with the group.

One drumming group after another carried their huge talking drums onto the field, and their rhythms filled the air. Often members of the audience stepped forward and danced to the music. It was a hot day, with unremitting sunshine, but nobody seemed to be bothered by the heat. Many performers and some of the audience were dressed in hand-woven kente cloth; the dust raised by all the activity could not dull the brightness of the colors.

Two of Akosua's brothers were members of the school choir, which sang several Twi songs. Some men did an acrobatic display, and throughout the afternoon two men on stilts strode and teetered across the field, making the children laugh.

The Asimhene gave a speech, praising Akosua for her work and for saving the lives of nobody knew how many villagers, and Akosua was asked to stand and shake hands with him. "I'm glad they haven't asked me to say anything," she said to him. "I know I couldn't."

The festivities continued until it was nearly dark, but before leaving, the chief of Asim spoke to Akosua and her parents. "We are so grateful that this village has escaped the smallpox epidemic. And we have you to thank, Miss Mensah. I remember as a small child, seeing members of my own family suffer from this terrible disease."

As the celebration concluded with a final round of drumming, Akosua felt elated, and she was determined to serve this community for the rest of her life. How could she know that her son's path would take her far away from the life she knew.